About the Author

DOVID KATZ, a native of Boro Park, Brooklyn, grew up steeped in the Yiddish of his father, Yiddish and English poet Menke Katz. After studying in Brooklyn yeshivas, he majored in linguistics (specialty: Yiddish) at Columbia University, relocating to London to write his doctorate on the origins of Yiddish. He established and for eighteen years led Yiddish studies at Oxford. After a stint at Yale, he settled in Vilnius (Vilna), Lithuania where he established Yiddish studies at Vilnius University. He has written prolifically on the history of Yiddish and has published four collections of original Yiddish short stories. He is at work on the Yiddish Cultural Dictionary (YCD). He is also a scholar and active opponent of the new East European Holocaust revisionism and edits the web journal Defending History. He divides the year between Vilnius, Lithuania and the mountains of North Wales.

About the Translator

BARNETT ZUMOFF, also a native of Boro Park, Brooklyn, known to his friends as Barney in English and Berl in Yiddish, was, in his 95 years (1926-2021) a US Airforce flight surgeon and brigadier general; chief of endocrinology at Beth Israel Medical Center and professor of medicine at the Albert Einstein College of Medicine; a leading figure in major secular Yiddish organizations in America. He was singularly dedicated to the survival of Yiddish and the capacity of its creative forces to appeal to the world at large. In that quest he became for many years the major translator of Yiddish literature into English, from the classics to contemporary authors, producing thirty volumes of translations. In 2012 he published a selection of Dovid Katz's stories of old Jewish Lithuania, and followed up with this, his last work, completed and sent to Noir in his final days.

Dovid Katz

East Broadway
to Whitechapel

Yiddish Short Stories

Translated from Yiddish by
Barnett Zumoff

Noir

Published by Noir Press Ltd
www.noirpress.co.uk
noirpress@hotmail.com
Company number 10622391

Cover design by Le Dinh Han

Cover illustration by Rimantas Dichavičius

Proofreading by Marija Marcinkute and Joy Collishaw
Typeset by Hewer Text UK Ltd, Edinburgh

Printed by Clays

978-0-9955600-7-9

Contents

Translator's Introduction

Yiddish Literature is one of the world's great literatures, in both quantity and quality. One of its unusual features is its compression in time: though scattered bits of the literature were published centuries ago, when the Yiddish language itself was going through its early formative stage, the bulk of it was published between the middle of the 19th century and the 3rd quarter of the 20th century.

The greatest figures in that literature, such as Mendele Moykher Sforim, Sholem Aleichem, I.L. Peretz, Avrom Sutzkever, H. Leivick, Yankev Glatstein, Moyshe-Leyb Halperin, Isaac Bashevis Singer, Chaim Grade, Mani Leib, Avrom Reisen, Kadya Molodowsky, Rokhl Korn, and Celia Drapkin, writers whom a current student of Yiddish Literature learns about, are all dead, and the tendency of both the students and the teachers is to describe Yiddish literature in the past tense.

However, it is important to point out that a significant number of Yiddish writers are still producing first-rate Yiddish literature today. One of them, Dovid Katz, the author of the present volume, is a master of the Yiddish language and the history of Ashkenazic culture, and he writes with equal familiarity and ease about European Jews of the last century or so and American and British Jews of today, the protagonists of the stories included in the present volume. I have put together a selection of his most interesting stories about contemporary Jewish life in the West and have undertaken to translate them in order to make them accessible to the current Jewish reader who does not know Yiddish. This volume supplements my 2012 anthology of his Lithuania-based stories, *The City in the Moonlight*. I hope that reading these stories will whet the reader's appetite for more of Dovid Katz's beautifully evocative tales.

AMERICA

Pride in Benjamin

A.

For hours, the little prankster with red side-curls lay hidden behind the green armchair in the corner of the living-room. The armchair was the most beautiful piece of furniture in the large wooden house in Brooklyn, but seldom did anyone sit on it, so Benjamin made that corner his lair. He would curl up quietly on the grey carpet behind the chair, with the easy patience of those compelled to do their own thing. Hiding away in a corner for hours accomplished nothing for Benjamin; it was pure mischief.

"If only he had as much enthusiasm for studying," they scolded him at school.

The evening his oldest sister, Feygi, was to meet a potential bridegroom from Israel, he had an even more burning desire to *see and be unseen*. There in the living-room was where they were going to have the *showing*, at which they would look each other over.

Benjamin had self-control that was not at all child-like. He understood very well that one yawn, one cough, one rustle would mean the end of his devilry. He had figured out how to lie as still as a corpse: pick something to look at and stare at the chosen object. So, he stared upward at the carved plaster circle around the old electric chandelier.

It was late afternoon on the frosty winter day in Brooklyn, but the house was too hot. The old radiator, of strong American cast-iron with carved decorations, stood right next to the armchair. Every now and then, a thin spray of steam would spurt out of a tiny hole and rain drops of hot water, as if from Noah's Ark.

The young suitor had flown in from Israel and was staying with their neighbours. His people had sent him to Boro Park, to a distant relative, a third cousin, so he could find a bride from Boro Park — from Brooklyn, not from somewhere in the colony of Monsey.

The Engelburgers were all in a tizzy. Feygi was past seventeen and there was no time for games. Her mother had her spend the whole day primping. They gave her a splendid hairdo: instead of her long braid, her hair hung down perfectly all around, almost like a girl's wig: above that her head was circled like a queen's by a green headband that sort of sparkled in a genteel way. Her long dress, which was light blue, was made of a silky material. They repeated to her advice on how she should talk to the young man and what she should ask him.

A quarter of an hour before the showing, as if by command of the Almighty, the chattering stopped. Everyone retired to his or her own room and sat there quietly. Aloud or under their breath, each one said a quiet prayer that the God of Sarah, Rebecca, Rachel, and Leah should shed His grace on Feygi, the daughter of Eliezer. Feygi herself was trembling with fear, a vague fear that she would sit there petrified like

Lot's wife and not say a single word. Her mother had left her a glass of Sabbath wine. She took a sip, and it did, in fact, make her feel better.

Meanwhile, the agile Benjamin had stretched himself out on the living-room carpet. He was sure he could hide, quickly and skilfully, as soon as any action started in the house.

The young man from Israel arrived, trembling with fear. He was skinny. His *khasidic* garments, which were too large for him, hung from his frame. His black side-curls were barely visible. He had a wispy beard that looked like tangled strands of black thread.

The Engelburgers led him to the living-room, where he saw a petrified Feygi sitting with her hands folded on the table. The parents immediately withdrew to the adjoining room and listened through the half-open door, not to catch every word but to get an idea of how it was going, to get some notion of what kind of creature the bridegroom was. After all, what could Feygi know about such things, and a marriage is not for just a few weeks. That very night they would know whether they were going to have an agreement or would have to *clean up a mess*.

The showing went swimmingly. They chatted for two hours, Feygi and the young man from Israel. Both were soon trying to figure out how they could bring the matter to a conclusion so her parents could talk turkey to the young man and send a telegram to his people in Israel.

Suddenly, the radiator, after a long period of quiet, started to spurt steam with a tsh-tsh-tsh-tsh rhythm, almost like the staccato *rosh hashone* blast on a *shofar** by an inexpert prayer leader. The young *khosid* from Israel had managed to suppress all his fears till then — the successful showing had filled him with the strength of Samson. He immediately sprang up to look around so he could show off to his bride that he knew how to fix things in the house, though he had never seen radiators or such cold weather in Israel. He leaned on the armchair with his left arm. Suddenly there was a scream — he hadn't noticed that a boy was sitting there all curled up on the floor, staring up at something.

A great commotion erupted in the house. Feygi's father rushed in, enraged, lifted up his youngest son, slapped him in the face, and yelled:

"You *sheygets!*"†

Benjamin didn't cry – neither from having his foot stepped on by the sad-sack from Israel nor from his father's slap; he had a roguish pride. But Feygi burst into girlish tears, sensing that all the womanly beauty her mother had put on for her that day had evaporated in the blink of an eye and had left her just a silly little girl sitting there crying. She said to the bridegroom abjectly:

"Don't have anything to do with us. What do you need with a family with such shame?"

The young *khosid* from Israel laughed and started trying to calm her, the way a husband would console his wife when she started to cry about something that was after all, not the

* Ram's horn—blown on *rosh hashone* and other auspicious occasions.
† Literally, a Gentile boy. Used as a disparaging epithet for a Jewish boy who misbehaves.

end of the world: "It's not so terrible, Feygi, and you can call me ' *dee* ' now," he said with a broad smile. "What is he – just a mischievous kid. But he does have a good head, doesn't he?"

"Yes, he does", answered Feygi, and from the depths of her sobbing a little girlish laughter slipped out.

None of this interfered with the match. After the wedding, Feygi often joked with her husband, who had come over from Israel to live with them in Brooklyn, about her little brother who had eavesdropped on their showing.

B.

In the Beth Yerukhim elementary school in Boro Park, they had had to put up with a lot from Benjamin Engelburger. He had not yet reached the age of *bar mitzve* but had already made as much trouble as a whole gang of pranksters. One time he took the elevated train to a store in Coney Island where they sold magic tricks. There he brought indelible chalk, and the next day he substituted it for the rebbi's regular chalk. When the rebbi tried in vain to erase the blackboard, the whole class erupted into diabolical laughter. Another time he brought a Beatles record and substituted it for the *khasidic* melodies they used to play on the holidays. Still another time, he set an alarm-clock to go off precisely at the time of the afternoon prayer.

---

* In standard Yiddish: "*du*". It is the familiar form of "you" in Yiddish, as opposed to the polite form, "*ir*". The young man is indicating that he wants his bride to speak to him at an intimate level, like family, and not a formal level, as between strangers.

People knew that he, the little rogue, was responsible for all those things, but they hadn't been able to catch him. No one informed on him either. To the boys he was a hero — he brought them joy. Besides, there's nothing worse among Jews than an informer. To his parents, he was their youngest son, and all the shameful things he did were offset by his clever sayings, which often made them laugh after a hard day's work on New York's East Side — they had a little store on Essex Street, where they sold cheap electrical appliances.

Little, skinny Benjamin Engelburger had a big, round face and big, black, round eyes that really didn't match his fiery red hair and the red side-curls that his mother curled every morning. On the other hand, his eyes did match his black pants, his black vest, and his black jacket. His face was ruddy and covered with reddish freckles. Gentile boys from the streets above 56th Street called him names, saying he looked like a Halloween pumpkin. It didn't bother him. The last Italian on his block, a genial pharmacist whose store was at the corner of 13th Avenue, actually called him tenderly, "My little pumpkin". In those days, a few Italians and a few secular Jews still lived on the same streets as the *khasidim,* whose leaders were gradually and methodically turning Boro Park into their world capital, 'Jerusalem of Brooklyn.'

Benjamin was eager to know what was going on with 'them'. He even sought out a non-religious friend, his name was Steve, whose house he used to sneak into from the back-yard to watch television secretly. The boys used to watch *The Three Stooges* and *Magilla Gorilla* together and roar with laughter. But once, just before *Purim,* when they were study-ing the *megile* of Esther, Benjamin yelled out *Magilla Gorilla* and the rebbe didn't like it very much. Steve's parents, who were teachers in a public school somewhere far away in Brooklyn, couldn't understand why a child should be forbidden to watch children's comedies on television. They considered that their allowing the little *khosid* to watch television was a contribution to liberal humanism.

Benjamin secretly played with two Italian girls his own age who went to a Catholic girls' school farther up the street. The girls wore their green uniforms and he wore his black one, and they played skelly with bottle tops and chalk-drawn squares on the sidewalk.

Benjamin made friends in the same way with all his forbidden friends. Other boys from Beth Yerukhim obeyed their parents. If someone who was not one of theirs said "Hello" or nodded their head to them, they would ignore them. If necessary to avoid appearing rude, they would give him a half-smile without looking. Benjamin, however, would promptly respond with a broad smile and a loud "Hello" that said, "Let's be friends!"

His people said that nothing good would come of that prankster, who was drawn to evil ways at such an early age. All Boro Park knew that the kid had eavesdropped at his sister's showing.

Benjamin's *bar mitzve* was small and cold, but he was satisfied with it. Becoming *bar mitzve* was a sign to him to become a real world-beater and ignore the chatter of older people.

C.

More than anyone else, Benjamin was curious about two Jews who were under a sort of unofficial ban of excommunication, though people weren't afraid of them. They were considered comical, half-mad fellows who even served to strengthen *khasidic* education by serving as an example to children of what sort of twisted thinking secular Jews could be led in to.

The first one was the *The Communist*, as he was called. He was short and fat, with thick, white hair that he combed out behind him and glasses with big brown tortoise-shell frames. He always had a pipe in his mouth, also tortoise-shell. He clamped the pipe between his blackened, tobacco-stained teeth. He took it out of his mouth only to speak. His gait was slow, like a turtle's, not like an old man's but proud like that of someone who did not lack self-assurance in any hostile environment. He lived alone in a basement apartment on 57th Street, which was then one of the border streets between the Jewish majority streets below it and the almost pure Italian streets above. Next to his door there always stood four large trash-barrels belonging to the four apartments into which the house had been divided, so it was easy to find him in the long row of similar houses.

The Communist used to spend whole days walking up and down the *khasidic* streets. He tried with all his might to converse with the religious children. His Galician Yiddish accent was not so different from the Polish-Hungarian Yiddish dialect of the children – it wasn't a Litvak Yiddish*,

---

* The dialect of Yiddish in Lithuania and vicinity.

which would have elicited cries of 'Lubavitsher heretic', or even worse, 'Misnagid.'*

But the children didn't respond to the man's "Good Morning" with even a hundredth of a smile, lest he would thereby convince himself that he existed and was walking around smoking a pipe and wasn't a Brooklyn mirage of a non-existent crazy person.

But in Benjamin The Communist sensed a friend, a boy who wasn't at all bigoted. A few days after Benjamin's *bar mitzve*, The Communist finally got an answer to his "Hello".

"Good-Morning, little boy!"

"Good morning, Mr. Jew!"

"I'm no Jew!"

"What are you then, a Turk?"

"A person! I'm a person! What's your name?"

"Benjamin. Benjamin Engelburger. What do you mean – isn't a Jew a person?"

"All the world's troubles stem from the fact that everyone keeps separate," said The Communist, taking his pipe out of his mouth and grimacing with disgust.

He made circles of smoke in the air with the pipe, and he pointed to each circle and gave it a name: "Poles, Russians, Romanians, Jews . . . Phooey! Feh! Together! Together, my young friend!" He lowered his hand with the pipe and put his other palm to his mouth and kissed it piously. He closed his eyes in reverence and said quickly and sedately: "Communism!"

---

* The anti-*khasidic* Orthodox Jews of Lithuania and vicinity.

Benjamin was a little confused. He said, half under his breath and half out loud: "A new kind of holiness!" and quickly ran away from the strange person, which was not at all Benjamin-like. He didn't understand what the man wanted from him, though he did understand, vaguely and obliquely, that the man's pushing the holiness and kissing his own hand was related somehow to the Communists in Hungary. People talked a lot about them.

Benjamin was drawn to speak some more with the strange Jew. A few days later they bumped into each other again.

"Good morning, Benjamin. Good morning."

"Good morning, Mister Jew."

"I'm not a Jew!"

"Excuse me, I forgot! Good morning, Mister Person."

"You're too thin, Benjamin."

"No, Mister Person, you're too fat!" Benjamin smiled broadly, with simultaneous dignity and audacity. This time, he wouldn't be afraid of the crazy old man.

"Let me teach you something about the body systems. When you're fat everything passes through you slowly. There's no rush. Your glands stay healthy. You think things through. When you're thin, everything runs through your body like a rat. Like a rat! You're nervous, you jump around, you can't think. Everything is zoom-zoom-zoom!"

"Good-bye, Mister Person."

"You're a good boy!" said the Communist, waving farewell with his pipe.

D.

Benjamin became the Communist's street-friend, absorbing another world. Boro Park was getting too narrow for the redheaded boy. There was one more ban of excommunication to violate and then the city would be his. Benjamin went over to New Utrecht Avenue, a broad, dark avenue above which elevated trains ran. In the dilapidated apartments there, poor people lived. The windows of the upper stories were at the level of the elevated tracks, and everything in those apartments would shake whenever the trains passed by.

Below, on the street, half the stores were abandoned and padlocked. In others, tailors, laundrymen, real-estate agents, and storefront lawyers hovered on the brink of poverty. People said that most of the so-called stores were fronts for Mafia hangouts. Children imagined that the back rooms concealed magnificent chambers where gangsters planned their adventures, and if they suspected that the police were coming, they would escape through hidden trapdoors into underground caverns deep beneath New Utrecht Avenue, where they kept glistening treasures stolen from distant lands.

But one show-window on New Utrecht Avenue was always freshly washed and sparkled with freshness. On the window was a painting of a small cross inside a larger Star of David. The four ends of the cross pierced the Star. Above it, in beautiful calligraphic lettering, was written in Hebrew: *"Jesus, the King Messiah."* Every few nights, someone would smash the show window. That didn't bother the missionaries — they would immediately send some of their people to bring a new show-window, with the same cross and Star of David and the same inscription. It was said that they had a hundred such show-windows in a factory somewhere — if they needed a new one, they brought it.

The missionary who ran the store lived in the back rooms. He was an old Polish Jew, thin and of medium height, with a completely bald head and thick, light-brown, youthful-looking eyebrows. He looked like some secular Jew from Europe, except that he wore a chain with a golden cross around his neck.

The convert, they called him in the neighbourhood. He too used to say "Hello" to every Jew on the street. The Boro Parkers didn't consider him anything like a Communist – when they passed either him or his store ('The Filth', they called it in the neighbourhood) they would spit three times and mutter under their breath, "Abomination of abominations – it is to be excommunicated!"

The convert used to stand on the sidewalk right in front of his store every day, looking for customers. In his twenty-two years there, innumerable Christians had come in but not a single Jew had crossed his threshold. That didn't bother him — Jesus had time and so did he! Now, he was quite aware that a redheaded boy had recently been passing by quite frequently. Finally, he spoke to Benjamin:

"Good morning, little boy."

"Good morning Mister Jew. Why did you become a convert? Repent! 'In the place where penitents stand . . .'"

"'. . . They outshine all the saints!'" the convert finished the quotation.

*　　*　　*

Benjamin stood dumbfounded. This was a plain, homey Jew! One only had to put a yarmulke on his head and lead him to the synagogue, and even though he had abandoned his beard and side-curls, he'd still be a *khosid.*

"Why do you have to be a convert? A Jew remains a Jew, you know. You are a convert, aren't you?"

"Little boy, what's your name?"

"Benjamin. You mean you want to be a person and not a Jew? You must be some kind of relative of the man from 57th Street."

"I have no family here in this neighbourhood. No acquaintances either. I work here to make Jews better Jews, true Jews who accept the Messiah."

"Jesus? He's lying in the ground with his feet turned backwards*! You don't know what *m'shumed* † means?"

"I know very well," the missionary answered calmly, "Let's see whether you know!"

"It's from *shmad, l'hashmid,* which means 'to destroy' ".

"No, little Benjamin. They've confused you with that nonsense there in your *kheyder*‡. The sinful Jews didn't want to accept that Jesus was the Messiah, so they deliberately left out the letter '*e*'."

"What '*e*'?"

"*M'shuemed!* The letter *ayin*, would make it clear that the word is from the root *omad*, which means 'to stand'. That

---

* In Yiddish, the words form a rhyming saying with a mocking tone.
† The actual Hebrew/Yiddish word for 'convert' is given here so the word-play in the next few lines can be appreciated.
‡ Religious elementary school.

means that they stood in the holy water of baptism and thereby accepted Jesus as the Messiah. Jesus, King of Israel! King Messiah!" And the convert kissed the air out of reverence and love.

"I won't talk to the rebbe about that," smiled Benjamin to himself. He was only interested in whether one non-believer would agree with the other.

"The man you say you don't know lives on 57th Street. He doesn't consider himself a Jew – he says everyone must be together, as people, and that there should be no Jews and no Gentiles. He constantly kisses his hand and says: "Communism!"

"A Communist? Communism is the number one enemy of mankind! They don't believe in God! They're the worst – murderers and blackguards!"

"I won't tell him that," Benjamin said, and continued down New Utrecht Avenue.

E.

Benjamin began to hatch a plan. He would become such a hero among Jews that the rebbes who used to consider him a mere prankster would confess that he was the greatest Jew in Boro Park. They would fight to make a match for him with the most beautiful girl in the world.

The next day, when Benjamin saw the Communist strolling along in the usual way, he didn't wait for him to start a conversation.

"Mister Person!"

"It's good that you call me that, Benjamin, very good! When you grow up, you'll see that the 'Mister' isn't necessary either. No titles! All people are equal! I love mankind! Mankind! I am old, but you will yet live to see a time when there will be no more Jews and no more Gentiles – only people! One mankind! Communism!" And he kissed his palm.

"Come take a walk with me! To New Utrecht Avenue! There's a Jew there – no, a person – that I want you to meet. OK?"

"I don't go to New Utrecht Avenue! A dark street! And the elevated trains clatter above your head. Boom, boom, boom!" He gestured three times in the air with his pipe. "But if Benjamin asks me to, I'll go there. Why not? Is he some religious nut or is he an intelligent person, this man?"

"If you come, you'll see for yourself."

"Slowly! Don't be in a rush! Slowly!"

The redheaded boy strode ahead of him by about ten steps, so people wouldn't suspect that he was going for a stroll with The Communist. That didn't bother the old man at all – he was happy with his new, young, religious friend.

When they arrived at the convert's show-window, the missionary didn't disappoint them. He was standing in front of his door. His eyes lit up when he saw that the redheaded young *khosid* was bringing him a secular Jew, apparently to have a chat with him, Messiah Jesus's emissary on New Utrecht Avenue. For a moment and in broad daylight, he had a vision that the truth of God and His only Son would finally become clear to a Jew from the neighbourhood. He had waited for this day, and now he had lived to see it!

The short, fat Galician Jew and the skinny, medium-height Polish Jew greeted each other warmly, with a plain "*Sholem Aleichem*" and its traditional reply, "*Aleichem Sholem*." Both felt rejuvenated, clearly sensing that they had finally found a person with whom they could hold discussions, one who wouldn't curse or pronounce anathema.

Benjamin moved into the background and disappeared, as it were, even though he still stood there leaning against one of the street columns that supported the elevated tracks.

New Utrecht Avenue was noisy. Gentile boys were screaming every possible English curse at one another. Suspicious-looking characters opened doors and looked around in all directions. Cars drove by. Up above, elevated trains rumbled by, sending down showers of splinters, steel, and sparks. Benjamin's ears ignored the tumult – he heard only the conversation between the two strange Jews for whom he had been the matchmaker.

"Are you from around here?" asked the Communist.

"Well, now I'm from around here," answered the convert. "I came here from Poland after the war. What else? And you?"

"Not far from there – south Poland"

"What kind of south Poland? If you came from Galicia, you should call yourself a Galitsyaner."

"We originally come from Vienna."

"All Galician Jews say they originally come from Vienna! Well as far as I'm concerned you have nothing to be ashamed of. Come inside!"

"What for? I'm just fine right here."

"OK, stay there."

"Is this your little store, with the cross in the Jewish Star?"

"It's not a little store! It's a mission to the Jews! Perhaps you don't know that Messiah Jesus was a Jew, that he was . . ."

"What kind of Jesus! What kind of Messiah! That's the same kind of crap that the fanatics in the neighbourhood spout. Where is he, that Benjamin? He's actually a good boy — we have to rescue him from them."

"Yes, we have to lead him to the Messiah!"

"What kind of Messiah! There is no Christ! There is no God! You all talk the same nonsense — this one talks about Moses, that one talks about Christ, and the other one talks about Buddha! There's only one mankind! Religion is poison! Poppycock! Feh!" And the Communist spat on the ground with the same pleasure as the *khasidim* who were constantly spitting on the sidewalk at the same spot.

"I have more pity for you than for the religious nuts from the Middle Ages that we have here in the neighbourhood. At least they believe in God! You've allowed yourself to be seduced by godlessness itself! Do you think the world created itself?"

"Give me a break! I know all about those stories. And who pays for all of this?"

"The Holy Church sent me here on my mission!"

"Parasites! You're a parasite too! You produce nothing whatsoever that can help mankind. No hungry people will be fed by your little store! No poor people will get a place to sleep! No . . ."

"It's not a little store! Hungry people need faith, not just bread!"

"Of course they need faith – faith in the truth, not in the lies of priests!" said the Communist, extinguishing his pipe and putting it delicately back in his pocket. He raised both hands to his mouth simultaneously, to give Communism a kiss.

Such paganism the missionary couldn't ignore. He grabbed the Communist's hands before he could press them to his mouth, like a priest who was trying to prevent someone in his flock from committing a mortal sin.

The Communist pushed him away with all his strength, pressed his index-finger to the painting of the cross inside the Star of David on the show-window, and shouted as loud as he could:

"This guy's completely crazy! One lie is not enough for him! For other people, one piece of foolishness is enough, but he needs two! He's a double fool! That's just what the world needs — Jews who believe in Jesus! Moses with his staff is not enough for them! Enough already with Jesus and enough already with Moses! Enough!"

The missionary, however, didn't allow himself to get excited:

"They've really seduced you good and proper! Bad attitude! May God have mercy on you! Jesus, the King Messiah, loves you with a deep love in spite of what you've said! He'll forgive you everything! Everything!"

"What doesn't exist cannot forgive! You yourself are the best example of how religion leads people off the tracks!"

"What tracks? There are tracks on the Elevated!" The missionary calmly pointed upward to the elevated subway line.

Their words multiplied and grew sharper. The two Jews were embroiled in the kind of heated argument that both had wanted. Two advocates, one for Christ and the other for Marx. They didn't notice that the redheaded boy was now surrounded by quite a large circle of *khasidim,* who took great pleasure in the amazing sight of each non-believer making hash of the other using all the criticism of this or that kind of Gentile and all the curses in the chapters of the Bible that describe the punishments awaiting Jews who do not obey God's commandments.

In the end, just two words rang out across the dark avenue and echoed back from the Elevated like some weird heavenly voice:

"Communist!"

"Convert!"

F.

The Jews talked among themselves about one thing and one thing only: a *bar-mitzve* boy had done this! Benjamin Engelburger! The immature prankster who had disrupted his sister's showing!

For many years in that district, they told the story at Passover *seders,* after "**khad gadyo*". The convert had attacked the heretic and the heretic had attacked the convert. People thought the world of Benjamin. They started to look for guidance from his tricks. He was a hero among Jews. The Engelburgers had lived to take pride and joy in Benjamin!

---

* The parable-like song that normally concludes the *seder.*

Eldra Don

A.

They said that Eldridge Street on the East Side was almost a
Jewish street. Why 'almost'? Because there, at number 17 –
an old building with nine apartments – there was a family
named Don, Spanish-speaking people from somewhere in
South America. Jose Don had worked himself up from an
errand boy twenty years ago to assistant director today in the
big furniture business Rappaport and Biegeleisen, there on
the *Galitsyaner* streets somewhere near Delancey Street.
Rappaport was long dead. Jose Don was getting near the day
when he would buy half the business and become a partner;
the business would then be called Biegeleisen and Don.
Partial fools kept their money in the bank – complete fools
bought stock on Wall Street. Jose had saved his earnings and
kept them in his apartment all those years. He was a carpen-
ter by trade and he built safe-storage boxes: one in the wall
behind the picture, another under the floor where the tapes-
try stood, and still another in the ceiling over the first hanging lamp. A few years earlier, everyone had lost everything in
the great Wall Street crash, but not Jose Don. And now, deep
into the Depression, the Dons were better off than their
neighbours. Mrs. Don had not had to work in years, and

their spoiled daughter, Eldra Don, had everything her heart desired.

All the eighteen and nineteen-year-old girls on Eldridge Street were called by their first names, but one girl was called by both her names, as if they were one: Eldra Don. Why Eldra Don was not just called Eldra no one knew. That's the way it was and that's all there was to it. Since a very early age, she had been a beauty. Her dark skin; her sensuous, always slowly moving lips; her large, round, dark eyes; her long black hair that sparkled in any light and seemed to turn blue – all of that excited any red-blooded guy once she was in her teens. She just had to be there and do her thing. Skinniness was not in fashion there; her magnificent breasts and full hips added no little bit to her attractiveness; her less-than-skinny forearms and hands also didn't hurt. She had one blemish: her teeth. Every tooth was more-or-less black. An upper tooth slightly to the left of centre was completely black. But that too only added to her desirability. When she sat down and her dress came up over her knees, they too had an attractiveness that was rare among knees. One didn't see her legs above that because Eldra Don always wore long, multi-coloured, loose dresses. They said she bought the dresses from Gypsies over on Clinton Street. Others said that her father got them free for polishing up the Gypsies' furniture that had gotten a little banged-up in transit, all with Biegeleisen's agreement.

Eldra Don spoke Yiddish pretty well. She had learned it while playing with the Jewish children in the neighbour-hood, though of course she couldn't read it. In her high school years, her friends were Italian girls who lived in Little

Italy further uptown; she couldn't stand the Jappy girls. The word 'Jappy' was attractive to the Jewish boys; they had modified it from 'Jap', an abbreviation of Jewish-American Princess, a half-refined, half-vulgar expression used for Jewish-American girls, thinking of them only half in jest as money-hungry-she-wolves who were only interested in one thing: "locking up" a boy who, when the Depression years were over, would become rich and would buy her a big house somewhere on Long Island. There she would lord it over her poor relatives who had remained in the city, showing them who she was and what she could do. She would decide who would have the honour of eating and drinking in her wealthy house on *rosh hashone* eve and, most of all, at both *seders*. She would give orders about who could bring whom to which *seder*, and everyone would know who was the boss in the family. Typical names of such Jappy girls were Susan, Karen, Beatrice and who knows what else.

The boys that this Eldra Don went with were usually Jews. For a girl who could attract any man on both sides of East Broadway just by existing, going with a Gentile was no big accomplishment, but having fun with boys who trembled about the scenes their parents would make because they were palling around with *shikses**, especially a dangerous *shikse*, one who spoke Yiddish even if it was with a Spanish accent – now that was an accomplishment. Eldra Don liked the word *shikse* very much. She wrote little English poems on that theme as homework in her literature classes in the last year of high school. She gave one such poem to her

* Unmarried Gentile girls.

teacher, a Jewish woman named Mrs. Applebaum, knowing very well that the teacher would get very upset.

> I am Eldra Don,
> Queen by night, Lilith by day,
> Eve at twilight, and to the end of my days
> A *shikse.*

> A gaze a sword, a word a spear,
> Spoken – captured, walked – lost,
> Touched – died, loved – betrayed,
> Sat *shiva**

> Pious, freethinkers, father, mothers,
> From fright – pale, from fear – feeble,
> Everything from me, the most *shikse-y shikse,*
> The black witch.

Mrs. Applebaum's custom was to ask all the students to come to the front of the classroom to read their compositions or poems to the class, but it was no wonder to anyone that she departed from custom that time, in spite of the fact that Eldra's classmates had been waiting for her recitation with bated breath.

B.

At that time there was a group of leftist Yiddish writers who organized a writers' association called *Tsifer-Blat* (*The*

---

* Seven-day mourning period after the death of a loved one.

Clockface). It was run by old newspaper people, former revolutionaries, mostly over the age of eighty. The ordinary members were new East Side writers, mostly poets who were between seventeen and twenty-five years old. There were absolutely no middle-aged people to be found there.

The chairman of *Tsifer-Blat* was N. Kredentz, who limped from a bullet wound he got during the failed Revolution of 1905. Exactly how old he was no one knew, but they said he would never see eighty-five again. When he gave a lecture on the occasion of Dovid Edelshtat's anniversary, he sprinkled his words with memories of his encounters with Edelshtat in London. When he gave a lecture about Ettinger, in that case without citing memories, people joked that he certainly remembered Ettinger, Mendelsohn, and probably King Solomon as well. Even without his limp, his gait was that of a terribly old man. But when he sat down and chaired a meeting of *Tsifer-Blat*, Kredentz looked a strong personality, a mighty master of words, with white hair that circled his round pate and a perfectly trimmed drooping mustache. He always wore a beautiful blue suit and a colourful tie. The meetings of *Tsifer-Blat* took place every Thursday evening and Saturday afternoon in a hall that the leftist principal of a local public high school 'rented' to it for no charge.

One Thursday afternoon, a group of senior high-school students stayed later for a rehearsal of the coming presentation at the graduation ceremony. Among them was Eldra Don. As she was leaving, she saw the group of writers who were waiting outside to begin their meeting as soon as the hall became vacant. These were not religious people – they were regular guys who spoke Yiddish as their natural language. Two of them were carrying a big red banner with a picture of a large clockface; instead of numbers, it had twelve pictures of tools – in the place of the 1, a hammer; in the place of the 2, a little wrench; in the place of the 3, a shovel; and so forth.

The hearts of the Jewish writers, the *tsiferblat-niks*, quivered collectively when the Spanish beauty with the gypsy-styled clothes came up to them. Some of the younger ones recognized her right away – it was Eldra Don from Eldridge Street. She was already an expert in pretending she didn't notice that everyone was looking at her. She went up to Aronowitz, a yellow-skinned, glasses-wearing, bony, little unattractive boy, and gave him to understand in Yiddish that she was not Jewish – that she knew how to speak Yiddish from Eldridge Street, and could she perhaps attend the meeting of the Yiddish writers?

L.B. Aronowitz, born in Foltitshen, Romania had been in America for about five years and, to put it mildly, had had no success with girls, was so shaken up by his unexpected good fortune that his four years among the leftists instantly evaporated. He stuck his hand in his left-hand pocket, where he used to keep a little *siddur** of his grandmother's, which, as a boy, he would squeeze when things were going badly. He began to babble. Drops of sweat appeared on his forehead. Finally, he managed a reply.

"Of course, why would anyone think otherwise? Our meetings are open to everyone. Come in!"

*   *   *

* A siddur is a Jewish prayer book containing a set order of daily prayers.

Kredenz banged his gavel on the table and opened the meeting in his usual way:

"Comrades, the 104th session of the literary association *Tsifer-Blat*, which fights for the growth of the Yiddish proletarian language, literature, and culture here on American soil, is now open."

At night, this Jewish man often dreamed that the police would disrupt a meeting of his and arrest everyone, and he slightly resented the fact that the government didn't give a hoot about him, his young comrades, or his words; by all means let the old man hold forth; New York City policemen had more important things to do.

At this meeting, the participants tried with all their might to carry on normally, but it didn't help. Eldra Don's presence and the rays of sexuality that glowed from her, without a drop of perfume, made everyone confused and nervous, from the youngest boy to the tried-and-true Kredentz.

One young man passed a note to his neighbour: 'Leyzer, I must tell you that the white stockings the Spanish girl is wearing are very attractive.'

Most of the young people recited poems, and some also recited excerpts from plays and stories. Afterwards, in the second half of the meeting, they conducted a 'critique', both about the things they had just heard and about things that had been published lately, first those that had been published in leftist circles, but then, in order to end in an elevated mood, they always closed with something that had appeared in 'rightist' circles. There things got jolly: everyone competed to see who could best demonstrate the mistakes and falsities of Yiddish writers who belonged to the 'Fascist', 'reactionary', and 'religio-clericalistic' forces, and who could best smear them with tar (really religious Jews and their writings were not even on their radar, not even to be mentioned.)

Eldra Don's Yiddish was a street Yiddish, charming and beautiful but without much grammar or 'difficult words'. She thought that all-in-all the meeting was a beautiful thing: young poets read from their poetry and people discussed and argued about literature. A lovely group. Even nicer was the fact that these were 'Internationalists'; here no one would bother her about not being Jewish. In addition, ninety percent were men. In brief, Paradise on the East Side.

Little Aronowitz recited from his latest play, 'Cousins', a story about four women, cousins, who all worked in a factory that manufactured men's belts. Aside from the few minutes when he was given the floor, Aronowitz spent the entire two and a half hours silently going over in his mind how he would invite the beauty for a cup of coffee at the moment that Kredentz would close with his "The meeting is hereby closed." He knew that the matter had to be carried out with military precision. A second too soon would show too much curiosity, as if it was planned in advance. A second too late and someone else would beat him to it and he would again be out of luck. In either case the chances were not great. He was not handsome. Everyone would run up to her. He would be nervous and talk nonsense, would blabber on, and would, in addition, have to suffer the embarrassment of seeing her leave with someone else.

Amid all the speeches and critiques, he could not free himself from thinking about his first defeat with a girl in

America: six months after his arrival in New York, his English was very weak, and when he wanted to ask a girl "Whether she would allow him to invite her out" he became mixed up and instead of using the English word 'permission' he said 'stepladder.' Where and how he got 'stepladder' into his head, he was never able to figure out. But he would never forget how the girl burst out laughing in his face.

When Comrade Kredentz finally banged down his gavel, Aronowitz methodically, as it were spontaneously and in an easygoing way, quietly asked Eldra Don whether she had enjoyed the meeting, and in the same breath he asked her whether she would like to have a cup of coffee in a café on Avenue A. He had thought out everything. What would be the use of inviting Eldra Don to the Café Europa? There the others would swarm around her like grasshoppers.

She agreed.

"Why not?"

"So, let's go!"

C.

Precisely that week, Aronowitz had a little money. He had done some translations from Romanian into English here and there for a publishing house in Bucharest. The two of them ran out of the hall before the others had a chance to interfere. In the heat of the 'operation', he left his manuscript of *The Cousins* behind. Someone gave it to Bialystok, the elderly secretary of the association, so he could give it back to Aronowitz the following week.

People were astonished how quickly Eldra Don had left with Aronowitz. It rankled the poet Z.Z. Dobkin most of all. Dobkin was not a little, ugly, yellow, bony, young man. He was a handsome fellow who always had to flee from the girls who came on to him. A tall, strong young man with black, curly hair and blue eyes, he had a soft melodic voice. The ladies called him Zizi, derived from his initials; no one knew whether they stood for Zelig Zalmen or Ziske Zanvil or Zevulon Zalkind. The other *Tsifer-Blatniks* liked this young man – he sent them girls.

Kredentz, Bialystok, and the other old men went home to sleep. Others left for various places. Zizi Dobkin and his clique, about fifteen young fellows, went to the Europa coffee house, not to discuss the new things that had been recited that evening but to discuss the miracle of our times: how and why and on what strength the ugly Aronowitz had gotten the beauty Eldra Don to quickly run away with him, that lout! Once they were seated in the café, they immersed themselves in the question.

"Just a minute – this matter has to be analysed properly. After all, she approached him even before the meeting, didn't she?"

"You're right – probably she liked him right away."

"Why are you knocking yourself out? He was standing closest to the students doing the rehearsal there."

"True – and she didn't want to give the impression that she had come to look for a boyfriend, so she went up to the nearest member and left with him."

"Maybe she knew him slightly from before."

"You know that or you're just talking?"

"What is the use of all this discussion – that's the way it happened."

"No – I myself saw how she took a few steps toward him. Such a beauty already has her own tricks – it's all theatre to excite everyone so they should start running after her."

"Brother – she's something worth running after."

"What have you all got against Aronowitz?"

"Nothing, but he is as ugly as death, so the whole thing makes no sense."

"So why do you begrudge him?"

"I don't."

Suddenly, the wealthy Zlata Berenholtz entered Café Europa. If her father had known that she was hanging around with the 'filthy Communists' he would have bashed her head in. Zlata knew Eldra Don from high school, and the men immediately told her what had happened that evening.

"In honour of your shared defeat, I will treat every one of you to a complete cure*. Prohibition has been repealed! You can drink even in the Café Europa. What'll it be? Cognac!"

"Bravo, Zlata! The saviour of the working class!"

"I don't see any working class – I only see a band of lazy young fellows who waste their years with foolish meetings. All of you, after all, are poor immigrants to whom America has given a home without pogroms, and instead of being grateful, what do you do? You propose revolutions and want to turn the country upside down! You should all be ashamed of yourselves! For Heaven's sake!"

"No, just the reverse – we think the world of America, and for that reason we want to turn it into a Socialist country."

---

* Colloquially used to mean a strong drink.

"What good are all of your stories – you're all lost. It's like *tisha b'av* mourning* here! And not because of capitalism, but because the Spanish girl left with Aronowitz. Where's Shloyme the waiter – come here, give everyone a glass of cognac at my expense. Put them all on my bill and take a couple of glasses for yourself."

"Bravo, Zlata!"

"Not for me," said Yosselson angrily (he was the most left-wing member of the group.) "I won't take gifts from some-one whose father, the exploiter Berenholtz, makes money from the sweat of his workers."

"Silly – my father works day and night to feed his family and the families of sixteen workers. And you? You chatter at meetings where there's a big, comical red banner on which there's a foolish picture of a clock and tools that is fit for a kindergarten. Such big shots! What fighters for a better world! Wow! Hoo-ha!"

Yosselson left. Nobody made jokes about the revolution at his expense! Zlata Berenholtz told the waiter to drink Yosselson's glass himself while the boss wasn't around. She turned to Zizi Dobkin.

"And what does the playboy, the Romeo, Dobkin, say? Zizi – speak! Why are you sitting there like a lump? No more big man, ha? I remember when any girl would have sold her own mother to get close to you. Ay, ay, ay!"

"Silly! Eldra Don is playing with us!" Zizi finally chimed in. "She approached the Romanian and left with him as a

---

* *Tisha b'av* is the anniversary of the destruction of Solomon's temple; it is a day of great mourning.

prelude to adventures in other circles. She expects all of us to run after her, and that's what she wants. I can assure you of one thing, Zlata: when such a beauty goes with the Romanian, it's with some kind of ulterior motive."

"What have you got against the Romanian?"

"Nothing. But why is that Aronowitz fooling around with Romanian translations all the time? He should work on his plays instead, so that at least something serious would emerge from it."

"You begrudge him for having work, ha? I think our Zizi is a bit . . . jealous?

"Definitely. Okay – that does it! What will you bet me that any of us who wants can go out with Eldra Don?"

The confident Jewish-American Princess answered without missing a beat: "If you can get a date with her, I'll give you a whole dollar!"

"Done!" Zizi drank down his glass of cognac in one gulp, his head tilted backward and his left hand holding on to the non-existent yarmulke so that it shouldn't fall off.

D.

Leybl Aronowitz and Eldra Don sat till eleven o'clock in the café on Avenue A. When it closed, they went to another café on the corner of East Seventh Street that stayed open all night. They talked and talked, enjoying the fact that they were speaking Yiddish. Eldra Don asked him to recite to her from his plays. He suddenly realized that he had left *The Cousins* in the meeting-hall. Usually that would have made him hysterical, but now, sitting at the little table with Eldra Don at one o'clock – to hell with *The Cousins!* It wouldn't get lost

– someone would return it to him on Saturday. He had in his breast-pocket a few pages of a brand-new play, *Artillery*, a comedy. He, yellow little Aronowitz, was reciting in the café, and she, the beauty Eldra Don, was hanging on every word, asking him questions when something wasn't clear. She was proud that a young Yiddish writer was reciting his work for her. That, she thought, was better than hanging around with the 'bums', as the Jews there called the common Gentile boys, especially the young Italian boys who lived farther uptown.

The matter between Aronowitz and Eldra Don proceeded apace. A week later, she was already staying in his furnished room on Division Street right next to Manhattan Bridge, where the subway trains clanged and screeched day and night. At first, Aronowitz turned pale when he recalled what a failure he had been with the four girls that he managed to seduce into bed in his lifetime: either he had been impotent, or he had come prematurely. The girls did not come back to him, and it didn't occur to him to even ask them. But, on the other hand, by God's miracle, the affair with Eldra Don went swimmingly. Apparently, she was no novice in the ways of love. She kissed him and caressed him for a long time, ruled the stubborn little fellow like a mother cat rules her kittens, and indeed called him "kitten." Eldra Don was the Mistress and Aronowitz was the Servant. Both of them arose from their love-play satiated, satisfied, and perhaps, one might say, in love.

This was all becoming a minor sensation. Eldra Don went everywhere with Aronowitz. He taught her to read and write Yiddish. For her birthday he gave her a present of Harkavy's dictionary – the new one, that is, with deluxe binding.

Jose Don was as immersed as ever in his business. In those years there were no customers in his neighbourhood, so he would 'export' furniture to Brooklyn, Queens, New Jersey, and even farther. He was constantly running around. Mrs. Don was a liberal person and had been some kind of revolutionary in the old country; the idea of her daughter going with a young European Jewish playwright had a certain charm for her. Aronowitz's parents were still in Europe, so that was not an issue. East Siders enjoyed it when things were happening. An old Polish Jew with a long beard, who used to spend his days sitting on a bench near the entrance to Kantorowitz's delicatessen, used to yell at the couple laughingly:

"Some match!"

A young rabbi on Hester Street only wanted to know when she was going to convert and asked her to promise that they would go only to him for the conversion and marriage instruction. Eldra Don always gave him the same answer:

"Don't worry. When we do it, we'll do it only with you."

People began to look differently at both Aronowitz and his plays. The humble, bashful ne'er-do-well had become a real bigshot. The *Tsifer-Blat's* publishing arm *Alarm* decided to publish *The Cousins*. They talked about putting it on on Second Avenue next season.

E.

Everyone was sure that at any moment Zizi Dobkin would try to ask Eldra Don for a date to regain a morsel of honour in his clique and also to get that dollar from Zlata Berenoltz. A whole dollar! But it didn't happen! Zizi Dobkin didn't interfere. After that evening in the Café Europa, he changed a lot. He became quiet, retiring, invisible. No one saw him, no one heard from him. He would rush away right after the meetings of *Tsifer-Blat*. His former clique, in which he was the central person, fell apart. Summer came, then Autumn, then Winter.

What Zizi really resented in the depths of his soul had nothing to do with girls; he resented that they were publishing *Cousins* as a book, a real book, and in addition they were going to put it on on Second Ave. He burned with writers' envy. Sitting in his lonely little room on Henry Street, he conceived a brilliant plan. Yes – that evening in Café Europa gave him the inspiration for his first book: he would write a book of poems that would be titled: *Eldra Don*. Poems scattered here and there in magazines get forgotten – who needs them! That's also true of just another book of collected poems. But everyone would talk and write about a long poem that would fill a whole book, a book about the Yiddish-speaking Spanish beauty who was bringing light to the dark East Side. That would be an eternal work about love, beauty, and friendship between peoples, a solution to the poverty and darkness and senseless antagonism between peoples that was the fare of all the big cities of the world.

Zizi slaved over his book day and night in his little room. He sent samples of his poems to an acquaintance in a Montreal publishing house. They accepted the book for publication. The gang in New York would know nothing till the bomb exploded. As he worked, he dreamed of the success of Z.Z. Dobkin's *Eldra Don*. There would be a meeting of *Tsifer-Blat*, where he, the young hero, would recite from his book. For months he imagined Aronowitz's face – how upset and angry he would be; how Eldra Don, hardly believing that he had written a book of Yiddish poetry about her, using her real name, would go up to him and declare her gratitude and admiration for him, Dobkin. Zizi's spiffed-up clothes for the meeting had been hanging ready for months on a nail in the door of his room. He had borrowed a bottle of cologne from a neighbour. The excerpts that he would recite, he had learned by heart – for dramatic impact, he would not hold the book in his hand. And about sixty years from now, he, the king of Yiddish poets, would write his memoirs and would then 'confess' that the inspiration for *Eldra Don* came from the fact that one evening in Café Electra the bourgeoise Zlata Berenholtz had made a bet with him for a dollar about whether he could get a date with the girl. He, the creative Z.Z. Dobkin, had bypassed the trivialities and had immersed himself body and soul in his work of true literature.

F.

Things at that time were going well again for Aronowitz. The first week they put *Cousins* on stage it was clear that it was a success with audiences. He received some royalties from it. He was also making more money from his Romanian translations. He had been going with his beloved Eldra Don for six months. You could say that the whole East Side was jealous of him. If you just hang in there, good things can still happen!

Someone knocked on the door. Aronowitz knew Eldra Don's knock very well. He ran to the door, opened it, and lifted her joyfully in the air. He immediately gave her a box of chocolates. Since he had had money to buy things, he had always kept presents for Eldra Don in the room. Whenever she surprised him, he also had a surprise for her.

"You wouldn't believe it, but someone has written a book about me in Yiddish!"

"What's that all about? When?"

"You know him. From *Tsifer-Blat*. Z.Z Dobkin. Actually, usually, I think they call him Zizi."

"Dobkin wrote a book about you? It was published? You saw it?"

"Yes, he sent it to me. With his autograph and a long inscription! A book called *Eldra Don*. My family in South America never thought that someone in New York would write a book of poetry in Yiddish about a child of theirs. A remarkable man, this Zizi Dobkin. Look at the first poem in the book."

> *I stand*
> *on the corner of the street,*
> *confused,*
> *in the evening,*
> *and sorrow covers stale creatures*
> *with little garbage-can lids*
> *and drips drops of iodine from the roofs.*
> *Through the steam from the street*
> *a swarthy mirage soars over East Broadway.*
> *With Shulamith's steps*
> *this dreary street is transformed*
> *into Semiramis's garden.*

Here, come see
sorrow dissolved
by the force of a woman
who strides throughout the city.
And I stand motionless,
as if in a trance in the desert,
and see, O man of the city,
O Eldridge princess, O Eldra Don.

"Look – that's only the first poem. A whole book about me! Imagine! Could you help me later with the difficult words? This is the real thing, not my kind of Yiddish, so to speak. Look – Zizi left a note in the book saying that the two of us should meet him today on the Williamsburg Bridge after supper, about nine o'clock. He invites us to have a drink with him in honour of his book. We should go, but I promised my mother to go with her to her sister's house on the West Side tonight. Ah, when my mother sees it! Unbelievable!"

"Go Eldra. I'll have a drink with Dobkin – Zizi – today myself to thank him and say congratulations, and I'll arrange a new meeting of the three of us, including you."

"Okay!"

G.

At a quarter to nine, Aronowitz was waiting at the Manhattan end of the Williamsburg Bridge. He looked down noisy Delancey Street. It seemed to him that the bridge was no more than a continuation of Delancey Street. The dirty waters below were open to everyone, whereas below Delancey Street people swam hidden in the tunnels.

Precisely at nine o'clock, Dobkin showed up. He was disappointed that Aronowitz was waiting there alone – that Eldra Don was not there.

"Good evening, Dobkin!"

"What can you tell me that's good, Aronowitz?"

"Things are Okay. Our beautiful Eldra Don will now have two Yiddish writers to choose from, in terms of literature, I mean. Of course, as for the rest, ha ha, we shall see, my friend. Look how beautiful New York looks from here," he said, turning around. "You can only see poverty from up close."

As soon as Dobkin turned around to look, Aronowitz pulled out a pocket-knife, not too sharp and not too big, and stabbed it into Dobkin's left side, methodically and quietly. The knife didn't penetrate too deeply, but Dobkin went into shock, froze like an ice statue, and let out a loud cry. Blood gushed from the wound. Little Aronowitz panicked – a group of people were still far away, but were rapidly approaching. He picked up the wounded man with superhuman strength, pushed him over the railing, and shoved him into the river. Dobkin let out a frightful cry that blended with the tumult of trains and autos and with the calls of the prostitutes nearby. Aronowitz immediately threw the knife into the river and walked very, very slowly to the other end of the bridge in Brooklyn.

The next morning, they pulled Dobkin's soaked and bloody body out of the river. A few hours later they found Aronowitz, dead drunk, in a Williamsburg courtyard in Brooklyn. He was immediately sent to Sing Sing.

The newspapers ran with the story. The whole city learned that a play by the murderer, a Yiddish playwright, would very soon be opening on Second Avenue. Tickets for the whole season sold out immediately, something unheard of in New York's Yiddish theater in those days. The agent would bring a full sack of money every week to Aronowitz's cell in Sing Sing. He distributed it to the guards and the other prisoners, so they would treat him not as a murderer but as the great playwright L.B. Aronowitz.

That Thursday, Comrade Kredentz conducted an evening of mourning in memory of the young poet who hadn't lived to see an evening in honour of his first book. His entire book, *Eldra Don* was recited.

Jose Don and his family moved far away, to another city. Nothing came of his dream to become Biegeleisen's partner.

The Solution from the Little Park

A.

Like secret lovers, they met in the little triangular New York park that was wedged into a space between buildings – giants all around. They argued and fought. Neither of them breathed a word about it to the members of his own family. The truth was that they were simply ashamed of their friendship.

Nevertheless, if they missed a week, it left them with a yearning that gave them a twinge, with the seething power of all forbidden human relationships. During the cold months, they didn't see each other at all. The first spring meeting every year took on the character of a linden tree, which in the old country was the first thing to revive and proclaim that spring was just around the corner.

At first, when they began to go down to the tiny park for a bit of afternoon relaxation, they couldn't make peace with their actions, in the New York way and the way of Jews from diverse tribes. The old, secular Jew, Abe Gilinsky, who had taken part in the uprising in the Vilna Ghetto, paid no attention to the reactionary who took the religious newspaper out of his briefcase every Thursday and immersed himself in articles and photographs of rabbis and rebbes. The young *khosid*, Mendy Kopelov, looked askance at the old Jew who took the secular newspaper out of his briefcase and read who-knows-what-kind of atheistic stuff there.

Old Abe Gilinsky was tall and thin, with a shiny bald pate, gold-rimmed glasses, and a carefully trimmed moustache. He was always dressed in a suit, a clean shirt, a multi-coloured tie, and newly shined shoes with tiny perforations, in the old-fashioned style. Young Mendy Kopelov, in contrast, was fat, with dishevelled dark hair, a dark little beard, and a black yarmulke that rested crookedly on his head when he took off his hat in the summertime and laid it down beside him on the bench. He was constantly straightening out his white shirt and sticking it back into his pants, but with almost every gesture the bottom ends of the shirt would pop out sloppily, as if of their own volition.

The first time they saw one another close-up in the little park, the old man from Vilna considered his afternoon neighbour a 'dirty *khosid*'. The latter, in turn, had secret contempt for the 'old heretic.'

In later years, when they talked about that early stage of their acquaintance, it was hard for both of them to remember how long that stage had lasted. But both of them remembered very well how it ended.

One Thursday, a breeze, which wasn't even a very strong one, managed to snatch away the religious paper from the young *khosid*. It flew out of his soft yeshiva-boy's hands. The breeze seemed to have pity on him and deposited it on the sidewalk nearby. The fat young man whirled clumsily, like a hurricane, grabbing for his flown-away paper, but the paper immediately won the contest with him. If his fingers were here, the paper was there, and when he got there, all the pages had been blown apart.

Looking on with a mischievous smile, the skinny old Jew with the bare pate quickly ran and took the blown-apart-broad-sheet pages in his hands. Slowly and quietly, he put them back in order, looking, meanwhile, with a contemptuous grimace at the pictures of the rabbis and rebbes. His face was imprinted with his thoughts: "Ugh! How primitive! There isn't a drop of progress there."

When he had put all the numbered pages in order, he handed them back to their owner on the next bench with a polite, worldly, European smile, and nodded to him, ostensibly with respect. Then he sat back down, in a dignified manner, in his usual place on the left bench, and again began to scan his secular paper with its tabloid pages.

At this point, the poor *khosid* was embarrassed. He was gasping as if he were exhausted, though his neighbour had done all the work. He didn't know whether to sit down or run away. He wanted to say thank you, but he didn't know how to carry out such a procedure, or, if he did so, in what language it should be. He stood there, confused, till his heavy body dropped with a thud onto his bench, on the right.

The awkward pause that ensued seemed to last an eternity.

Finally, the old man got up again, politely and elegantly, and proffered a firm handshake to the pious Jew. He didn't say *Sholem Aleichem* but introduced himself New York-style:

"Abe Gilinsky. How do you do, young man."

"M-my name is M-Mendy, Mendy Kopelov," the *khosid* stammered.

"Where are you from?"

"From Brooklyn. My parents are from Bobruisk, in Russia."

"Bobruisk is considered *White* Russia. In the old days, hardly any Jews lived deep in Russia," the old man corrected him pedantically.

"If you say so. We consider it all part of Russia. From your accent, you seem to come from the same region, isn't that right?" Mendy asked, recovering somewhat.

"I'm from Vilna – I was in the Vilna Ghetto."

And in that instant, Mendy lost any disrespect whatsoever for the old man.

"So – goodbye!" said old Abe Gilinsky with authority.

He put his secular paper back into his briefcase, stood up, and went back to his jewelry store, which was a few blocks away. Mendy sat for a while like a lump, and finally left to go back to the office where he worked, on a high floor of a nearby skyscraper.

Abe Gilinsky, who had once been a student in Ramayles yeshiva in Vilna before it was destroyed in the war, had wondered for a long time how these *khasidim*, whom one had barely been able to find in Vilna, had established such a big new generation here in America.

At the same time, Mendy Kopelov wondered how such a fine, upstanding Jew from Vilna, a war hero in the fight against Hitler, could abandon *yidishkayt** for that *worldly*

* All things Jewish, Jewishness.

nonsense – which is what they called everything related to secular Jews in his house.

The next few times they were sitting in the little park at the same time, they were already greeting each other more and more warmly, and casting glances at each other that seemed to say: Let us be friends.

B.

In the course of the next few weeks, the two men met a number of times in the tiny New York park, the skinny old reader of the secular Yiddish newspaper, Abe Gilinsky, and the fat young *khosid*, Mendy Kopelov. Since Abe had rescued Mendy's religious paper from flying away in the breeze that Thursday afternoon, they had greeted each other and grown closer and closer to the yearned-for discussion that both of them were very curious about, as if it was some evil passing thought.

They had their first discussion on a hot day. Years later, Abe Gilinsky recalled that it was in the days close to the American holiday the Fourth of July, which to both him and his friends was a tremendous symbol of freedom for all mankind. Mendy Kopelov remembered it as the 17th day of Tammuz, when religious Jews fast to mourn the day that Nebuchadnezzar's army broke through the walls of the holy city of Jerusalem, over 2500 years ago.

Despite the June New York heat, Abe Gilinsky showed no signs of discomfort. As always, he was wearing his tie and hadn't opened the top button of his shirt. Mendy Kopelov was sweating as if he were in a steam-bath; as always, he was wearing a white shirt buttoned all the way up, without a tie.

"Tell me young man. Which *khasidic* group do you belong to?" asked Abe, using the familiar *'du'* to his young neighbour in the park.

"Chabad!" Mendy answered proudly.

"Really? We hardly saw any members of *Chabad* in Vilna. Seems to me that the Vilna Gaon* and his people drove the *khasidim* out of the city."

"The old Rebbi came to Vilna to make peace. What was he to do if the Gaon was away from the city at just that time? He had left the city because simply not receiving the old Rebbi, such a great scholar, was something he wouldn't have been able to do."

"Which old Rebbi? The Baal Shem Tov? Nachman Bratslaver?"

"No – the old Rebbi was Reb Shneyer-Zalmen of Lyadi, the founder of *Chabad. Chabad,* you know, stands for *Chokhme* (wisdom), *Bine* (understanding), and *Da'as* (reason).

The word 'Rebbi' grated somewhat on Abe Gilinsky's ears, because the young man pronounced it with an American 'r' and a sharp 'i' at the end. This was not a *rebbe* from the old country!

"Okay, okay, okay! Listen to me, young man. I have nothing against your 'Old Rebbi', but that was hundreds of years ago when there was no freedom, people lived in darkness, and Jews had no education."

---

* A great Jewish scholar who was the spiritual leader of the *misnagdim,* the anti-*khasidic* Orthodox Jews of Lithuania and vicinity. He led the group of great rabbis who excommunicated the *khasidim . . .*

"Darkness? *Yidishkayt* casts the most beautiful light! When our previous Rebbi, Reb Joseph-Isaac, was rescued from Hitler, he came here to New York on a Tuesday, on the 9th day of Adar, in 19—"

"I certainly have nothing against him for being rescued – would that everyone had been rescued – but *we* fought against the Germans with our last ounce of strength. Even the Communists fought. Your people went like sheep to the slaughter. In many villages, the rabbi even told the Jews to obey the Germans and go willingly into the grave! Tell me, really, young man – I mean it as a serious question: how can one continue to believe in a God who was so bankrupt?! Who utterly failed us?! If He existed, would He, our good friend the great God, have been silent when they slaughtered all the Jews? The *khasidism* and the *misnagdim,* the Socialists and the Communists, the Labour Zionists and the Revisionists, the, the – – –" *

"If the Jews had remained faithful to the Almighty, faithful to the Torah that God gave the Children of Israel in the desert and hadn't gone along with the foreign lifestyle that just happened to be popular among the Gentiles, it wouldn't have come to that! It wasn't the *khasidim* in Russia and Poland who made Hitler into such an Amalek†, it was the influence of the foolish German Jews. They thought that if they imitated the Germans they would be accepted. They thought – – –"

* The speaker is citing pairs of opposing factions among the Jews.
† A tribe of fierce enemies of the Jews (in the Bible); symbols of all enemies of the Jews.

"You should be ashamed of yourself! You dare to blame the innocent victims that the Fascist murderers slaughtered? Feh! You're ready to say such idiotic things to help your God, the 'Almighty' as you call him, worm his way out of this? Ha! With such an Almighty, it's no wonder that there's darkness down below!* And you pray every day, yet, to such a God. Where's your common sense? Huh?"

"Reb Abe – what should I call you? What's your Jewish name?"

"It was Avrom, but I'm no 'Reb'. I was once a student in Reb Mayle's yeshiva, which we in Vilna called Ramayles yeshiva. Thank goodness, I got away from there! Abe – that'll do! And what's your name? Seems to me you called yourself Mendy when the paper with the pictures of the rabbis flew away from you. Probably the Almighty did that too."

"Everything comes from the Almighty. They call me Mendy. When I'm called to the Torah, it's Menachem Mendl, son of Reb -"

"You're really a Menachem Mendl[†]! What am I saying – your people are not even *allowed* to read Sholem Aleichem! 'A danger to your morals,' *'treyf'*[‡] and impure.' Right?"

"What's this 'reading *Sholem Aleichem*'? I don't understand what you mean. *Sholem Aleichem* is what you say to a Jew when you shake his hand."

---

* A play on words; the Yiddish for 'Almighty' is *'der eybershter,'* which literally means 'the highest one' or 'the one farthest above,' hence the contrast between 'above' and 'below.'

† A character in a Sholem Aleichem series, who was a folksy wanderer who was constantly indulging in new, usually unsuccessful attempts to make a living.

‡ Specifically, non-kosher; more generally, impure.

"You don't know such a famous Jewish writer?"

"Let him be famous till 120 years of age! How can I have anything against him if I don't know what he's written? A heretic, probably?"

"Till 120 years?! A thousand-and-one nights!" Abe Gilinsky looked away from the young man and talked to the air. "He doesn't know who Sholem Aleichem is, doesn't know that he died in nineteen sixte------"

"All right! Blessed be the departed! Did his children say *kadish** for him? Or don't you believe in *kadish* either?"

"Doesn't it get boring for you to stay in the tiny world of your Rebbe?"

"Tiny world? Our Rebbe, may he live a long life, is the greatest man of our time! His interests encompass everything! Incidentally, he also studied philosophy in France, but that's irrelevant. The Rebbe's love of *yidishkayt* has warmed the souls of Jews throughout the world. My friend – no, Abe, Abe. Did you put on *tfiln†* today?"

On hearing that, Abe Gilinsky's serious expression dissolved, and he burst into laughter.

"*Tfiln*? Such a nuisance is all I need every day! Tsk Tsk Tsk!"

"Oy! You mustn't! It's the law of the Torah – - that means the Torah says – - – "

"I remember very well, young man, what 'law of the Torah' means!"

---

* Prayer said by those mourning a deceased person.
† *Tfiln* – Yiddish for phylacteries, small leather cases, containing scrolls with sacred Biblical passages, worn by Jewish men at morning prayer.

"That's certainly good! So, if you remember, what have you got against putting on *tfiln*? If you put on *tfiln* – – – "

Abe Gilinsky couldn't contain himself. His laughter again boomed out over the park.

"Listen here, Abe! Laugh all you want – – God bless you! But I'm going to bring down a set of *tfiln* and – – – "

"Bring them down and get all mixed up in the leather straps yourself! Put on a yoke with harness straps too. What do I care!"

"Yoke? Shafts? What are you talking about? Those aren't harness straps in the *tfiln*, they're str – – – "

"Yes, yes, I know, I remember, of course – strips of leather. Take them away, your leather strips, to Boiberik*! No, to Bobruisk! To Baranishok! It's all old-time superstition. Do you think that civilization has stood still, young man?"

"What do you believe in? Tell me, Abe, please – I'm curious. In what do you believe? In Communism? In what? Do you believe the world was created by accident?"

"What Communism? We, the real Socialists, we have fought against Communism all these years! Now that the disgusting, Stalinist Soviet Union has collapsed, it's a holiday. We Socialists fight for freedom! Equal rights! Justice for all people!"

"A 'holiday' yet! And what do you call such a 'holiday' (not to speak of it in these same breath as a real holiday)?"

"Don't talk foolishness, all right? We secular Jews have our holidays! The first of May is a holiday!"

---

* Mythical resort city in Sholem Aleichem's writings.

"What kind of holiday is that? Between *peysakh* and *shevues*? It might come out on *lag b'oymer*!" said Mendy, starting to feel his oats.

"*Oymer, shmoymer*! Wake up, young man! It's the holiday of the workers. Thanks to the workers, you have what to eat, young man, though I assume you've never worked. And thanks to the workers, you have what to wear."

"I still can't understand your answer about your faith."

"I believe in Democratic Socialism. That's not a 'faith', as you call it. I believe in the equality of all peoples, in the full freedom of everyone to believe whatever he wants to, in the rights of the workers against the power of evil, against – – –"

"So why do you need Democratic Soshism, whatever you call it. Forgive me, I'm not well versed in worldly matters."

"It's not a 'worldly matter,' it's the foundation of human society, of a peaceful earth, and of pluralism! Thanks to pluralism, you can live your life with your *khasidism* and no one bothers you. For you, that alone should play a large ro – – –"

"Wait a minute! Again, I don't understand. As far as being on the side of the poor, it says in the *mishne:* 'Love work and hate the bosses.' That means – – – "

"I know what it means. In the ancient Scriptures, you can find all sorts of things – good things, wise things, and also horrible things."

"What can be horrible in the Holy Scriptures? What? Do you have an example? Do you have *one single* example?"

"That for all kinds of transgressions you have to be killed: 'He shall surely die', it says."

"But you see that we don't kill anyone these days. The Talmud has come along to interpret – – – "

"Aha! I know – I've heard that story before! Twisting things around; what do you call it – *pilpul*,' hair-splitting. By splitting hairs, you can interpret that 'an eye for an eye' doesn't mean an eye for an eye – it means money. You see?! *Your* rabbis, not mine, couldn't stand the barbarity of the Bible, so they had to interpret everywhere and make excuses!"

"Oh God in Heaven! May He forgive you for what you are saying!"

"If He existed, it's you He would have to forgive for blaming the victims and exonerating the Nazis."

C.

They argued constantly, these two Jews – the old secularist and the young *khosid* – when they met during the warm months in the tiny triangular New York park that was wedged between the skyscrapers.

It wasn't long before they began to bring each other 'gifts'. Actually, they were given with ulterior motives, as weapons in the debate. Neither Abe Gilinsky nor Mendy Kopelov believed he would change the other's mind, but what then? It was important to each of them to diminish the other's antagonism, even if only slightly. The secular Jew gave his fellow-discussant a collection of Bashevis Singer's stories (though Bashevis Singer was far from his favourite writer). The *khosid* gave his fellow-discussant the first volume of the 'Book of Discussions', by the previous rebbe, the learned Reb Joseph-Isaac.

The holidays passed. The days started to get colder and they no longer visited the little park. Both hid the *'treyf'* merchandise carefully in their houses, so the other members of the family wouldn't find out that they were reading unsuitable things.

After several months had passed, both of them – the old man in the Bronx and the young man in Brooklyn – began to read the secret gifts. Both enjoyed them very much. The *khosid* was astonished that the Yiddish writer was so deeply immersed in the *yidishkayt* of the old-time Polish *shtetls*. The secularist was very taken with the previous Lubavitcher Rebbe – that as soon as he arrived in New York from burning Europe in 1940, he immediately told the American Jews that they weren't doing enough to rescue their brothers in Poland: "As far as I understand the average, naïve, American Jews in general and the atmosphere in which Jewish community activists live in general, I'm sure that not only can they not imagine the murderous behaviour of the beastly, evil German but that they have no desire to believe the murders that are taking place, let alone understand the thoughts of a Haman* – – –"

When spring came, the meetings in the park started again. They debated the books exhaustively and exchanged new gifts: One time a volume of Zhitlovski, as an example of a great secular Yiddish scholar, and another time a volume of Sholem Aleichem, with the ideas of the Baal Shem Tov in Yiddish.

---

* An evil minister in Persia, in the Book of Esther, who wanted to kill all the Jews in the kingdom.

Their arguments now assumed the character of those between friends who are discussing their differences, one with the other. The old man habitually used *du* while the young man stuck with *ir*.

D.

Those were the days when the Lubavitcher Rebbe, Menachem Mendel Shneeerson, lay gravely ill.

The ill-will of Abe Gilinsky toward the Lubavitcher *khasidism* was pretty deeply ingrained. As a *misnagid* child in Vilna, in Ramayles yeshiva, he had heard nothing good about them. After turning secular when he was still young, there was no longer anything to talk about. And in America, he considered the 'crazy Jewish missionaries' who annoyed Jews that walked the path of modernity and strove to 'catch young souls' no different from any other American cult.

Now, however, against his will as it were, he had a young friend who was a Lubavitcher *khosid*. And in the days of the Rebbe's grave illness, he began to have empathy with Mendy, admiring how much real human emotion and love young Mendy had for the Rebbe. His thoughts turned to his own two grown children, a daughter and a son, who took a dim view of their father for reading a Yiddish newspaper, going to too many Jewish events, and still considering himself a Socialist.

Then the Rebbe died. All the New York newspapers wrote about it. In the New York Times, there was a long article, with a photograph of a Lubavitcher girl crying her eyes out.

Mendy no longer showed up in the park. Their places of work were only a few blocks from one another, but go look for someone in New York! It was as if they had worked out the rules of a forbidden friendship: don't ask each other about their job, their trade, their family, their address – nothing. They met, not so much in a space between buildings as at a point in time, space, and history.

Abe assumed that Mendy had found some other job, and that was that! He missed his young friend, who was the only young person in America with whom he had spoken Yiddish.

"Even if it's someone to argue with in Yiddish, that's good too," he thought to himself.

About a year later, on a hot day in July when Abe Gilinsky was sitting alone in the little park, he sensed someone standing right next to him. He looked up. It was Mendy Kopelov. Abe stood up and hugged the chubby Lubavitcher *khosid*.

"Where have you been hiding? I was worried!"

"I wasn't hiding. After the Rebbi's – – – "

"I know – – – "

"The third day of Tammuz is the anniversary of his death. A year has passed already without the Rebbi. The end of *shabes,* on the third day of Tammuz in 1994, is when the catastrophe occurred."

Abe Gilinsky was filled with respect for his old/new friend. He couldn't help but admire the devotion and love, and a thought slipped out that he immediately regretted uttering:

"If our young people had that kind of a relationship to our writers and leaders, things would look different for us today."

Mendy said nothing. His mourning and sorrow had killed his passion for debating.

But Abe immediately returned to his argumentative, hopeful mood toward his young friend from the park, as if not a day had passed since their meeting a year earlier.

"It was in all the papers that you Lubavitcher *khasidism* believe that your dead 'Rebbi' is the Messiah, and that at any moment he'll be resurrected from the grave. You believe about him the same thing that Christians believe about Jesus, about whom the old-time Jews used to say: **"nit geshtoygn un nit gefloygn."*

"No, no!" Mendy protested in a whispery voice, nothing like the contentious voice he had used previously. "There are crazy people everywhere! A tiny group have gone off their rockers! It's an insult to the Rebbi, of blessed memory. He himself would never have allowed it. But that's precisely what they choose to write about in all the papers – *that's* the real blasphemy!"

"So let me tell you what – I'll explain the matter as I see it. It just took longer in your case than with the Holocaust in our case to lose the spirit of your movement. Whether it's an American-born or an Israel-born Rebbe, it won't be the same! Not the same, my young friend! Your Rebbe, though I didn't agree with him, had all the charm of Yiddish, of *shtetl* Jews from the old country. All the Jews of Eastern Europe, regardless of what group they belonged to, regardless of their convictions, had a real, deeply ingrained spirituality, an immersion in larger issues, a belief in *something*.

---

* Literally, 'he didn't rise and he didn't fly', expressing disbelief in the resurrection of Jesus. Used figuratively to mean something that makes no sense or is unbelievable.

Whom will you install as the new Rebbe, an American rabbi who is also interested in insurance? Your people themselves know it wouldn't have the right feel!

"Because of the Holocaust, you don't have any people with the true character of the old country and that has led your colleagues to go crazy! The Messiah, indeed! He's as much the Messiah as I am Buddha! Or Mohammed! Cut the nonsense!"

After a long silence, the young Lubavitcher *khosid*, Mendy Kopelov, responded to the old secularist Abe Gilinsky's accusation that after the death of the last East European-born Rebbe they would now be unable to accomplish anything.

"Why should I deny it to you? Without the Rebbi, things are very bitter. What can I do about those crazy people prattling nonsense, that the Rebbi is the Messiah?"

"Listen, Mendy – enough about the crazy people, the 'Messiah-ists' among you. I have belonged to various movements in my time – what will your movement do without a Rebbe?"

Mendy didn't like the sound of the word 'movement' applied to *Chabad*. Nevertheless, he understood the essence of Abe's question.

"Listen, Abe, you're a man of the world – give us some advice! What do we do!? Where do we find a Rebbi after the last Rebbi?"

"A difficult *halokhe**, as they say," Abe responded, using that expression for the first time since he had come to

---

* Figuratively, a tough question. Literally, a hard passage of *halokhe* (Jewish Law) to interpret.

America just after the war. "Listen, my young friend, we differ in our world-views, *'hashkofes'* I believe you call it in your circles, but nevertheless we are friends. I'll tell you the unvarnished truth – I missed you! A friend disappears for a year – imagine that!"

"I missed you too."

"It's time you called me *du.*"

"Done!"

"Listen, Mendy, I'll think about what the Lubavitcher *khasidim* can do under such circumstances. But don't disappear for a year!"

"I'll be here tomorrow, God willing, and we'll talk some more."

When Mendy arrived in the little triangular park the next morning, he found Abe looking pale, with an open collar. His tie was slung across his shoulder. The old secular Jew was ashen-faced.

"Mendy, you won't believe what happened to me yesterday! After our meeting, I spent the whole day thinking about what the Lubavitcher *khasidism* should do now that their Rebbe has died on them. I couldn't figure anything out. But in the middle of the night, when I was sleeping, I dreamed – and let me emphasize that it was only a dream – in my dream, there came to me – you won't believe this – none other than your ancient Rebbe, Shneyer-Zalmen of Lyadi (in the yeshiva where I studied in Vilna, they called him, simply, the man from Lyadi). In any case, here's what he told me when he came to me in my dream:

'Reb Avrohom, son of Reb Zalmen Isser! You are a hard-necked *misnagid* who later left *yidishkayt* completely, but

you fought heroically against the evil beast with your heart
and soul and body and life, and *you* are the one I have
selected, and it's to *your* dream that I've come so you can
announce my true will to your young friend from Chabad
and he, in turn, can announce it to whoever the right people
are in the movement.

'The departed Rebbe, our leader Reb Menachem Mendel
Schneerson, blessed be the memory of the righteous one and
may his great spirit reside with us, was a son of Leyvi-
Yitskhok, who was a son of Borukh-Shneyer, who was a son
of Leyvi-Yitskhok, who was a son of Borukh-Sholem, who
was a son of Dvoyre-Leye, who was a daughter of my son
Dov-Ber, who moved his realm and his court from Lyadi to
Lubavitch, where Sholem-Dov-Ber later founded the
Tomkhey Temimim yeshiva. Remember – from Heaven
they can see everything – they can see it all!

'As for the pygmy American rabbis who are quarrelling
about Menachem Mendel's will, including all those whom
the foul spirit of Sabbatai Tsvi* has entered, God have mercy
on those who say that the departed Rebbe Menachem
Mendel Schneerson is the King Messiah and will be resurrected. Those are just foolish words that lead to blasphemy
and let people compare the sons of *Chabad,* God forbid, to
the followers of Sabbatai Tsvi, may he *absolutely* not be
spoken of in the same breath!

'The new Rebbe must be from my family, from the house
and seed of Shneyer-Zalmen, a true Schneerson. So let my
khasidim, the sons of Chabad, start searching everywhere,

---

* A self-proclaimed false Messiah in the 17th century.

from Alaska to Jerusalem – till they know immediately, from his radiance, charm and wisdom, that he's the one. Whether he's an ignoramus, or even a heretic, makes not the slightest difference.

'If he's the right one, he'll be willing to learn the basic ideas. Let them bring him to the *Tomkhey Teminim* yeshiva of your times and let him only then become a great scholar – the fact that he, like Rabbi Akiva* had been an ignoramus up until then would be irrelevant. Let him study Torah and the religious lifestyle for ten years, twenty years, not making a splash, till it is obvious that he is worthy of the ruling crown, and then let them make him the Rebbe of the House of Chabad. So go and fill your horn with the oil for anointing, and go look for the new ruler from the house of Shneyer-Zalmen, a man from the Schneerson blood-line, and anoint him immediately, though only later will he rise to the ruling position. And if there are two, then look into their hearts and not at their appearance – as it is written: 'It is not what a man sees with his eyes but what he sees with his heart.' For it is not what a man looks like – man looks at appearance but God looks at the heart.

'Give my regards to your young friend from *Chabad*, for he was born for this holy mission, and you were born for this holy mission. And the Almighty will grant your family health and happiness. Thus is His will.'

* A renowned rabbi who was the mentor of Bar Kochba, leader of the second Jewish revolt, in the 2nd century. C.E. He came late to the rabbinate, and had been an ignoramus till then.

Mendy Kopelov stood petrified, like Lot's wife. He felt as if an angel from Heaven had made him a holy emissary, almost the way God sent the prophet Samuel to Jesse in Bethlehem.

That night, Mendy went to 770 Eastern Parkway in Brooklyn* for evening prayers, and told the Lubavitcher rabbis about what Shneyer-Zalmen had said when he came to the dream of his friend Avrom Gilinsky.

Word spread through Chabad circles, that here was the solution to the riddle. A way out. An answer. Salvation.

Mendy told them all about the meetings in the little park. They fretted about the fact that Reb Shneyer-Zalmen had chosen to come in a dream with the solution, and not to a Lubavitcher *khosid*, nor even to a religious Jew, but, almost as if by divine intention, to the secularist Abe Gilinsky. They considered the matter deeply.

And, very quietly, the sons of Chabad began sending their emissaries to all corners of the earth to search out the descendants of Shneyer-Zalmen, in the Schneerson bloodline, in order to find and anoint the future new Rebbe.

And when they found him, he was a very young and openminded fellow who had been searching far and wide for higher truths. They immediately convinced him to leave his country, his family, and his job and go study in the *Tomkhey Temimim* yeshiva. There he is quietly studying to this day. Only a few able, senior individuals from *Chabad* know who

---

* The world headquarters of the *Chabad-Lubavitch* movement.

he is, know that they'll make him the Rebbe someday, when the time is right. Among themselves, they already call him 'the new Rebbe.'

And among themselves, when they talk about the matter and don't want others to know what they're talking about, they refer to it as *the solution from the little park.*

Lenore

A.

Lenore Wineapple went home to Brooklyn on the eve of *khanike*. The train stopped with a screech on the *El*,* the rails that stood high in the air over McDonald Avenue. When the doors opened, the cold outside was piercing. A group of sweaty, exhausted passengers, back from a day's work in New York, immediately began to push and shove to get off the train and onto the wooden platform, and then down the stairs, which shook from the train above and the shoving below.

Below, in the street, on the sidewalk right next to the subway steps, a grey kitten with four white paws was washing herself as if she were sitting in a house on a carpet next to a warm fireplace. A short man wearing a peaked cap shoved the kitten aside with his right foot. Either he had wanted to save it from the rushing feet and shoved it too hard or he wanted to punish the animal because it was sitting practically right in his path; in any case, it was more of a kick than a shove. A pretty young Italian girl wearing tight dungarees decorated with two fashionable patches, one on her left

---

* Refers to the elevated train lines in some parts of New York City.

buttock and the other on her right, quickly bent down, picked up the now limping and wailing kitten, whispering to it: "You're coming home with me," and raced home even faster so the good deed wouldn't delay her for even a minute.

Lenore bought an evening paper from an old black man, known locally for his elegant grey, unusually square-shaped moustache, who usually sat on a chair right next to the subway steps and sold newspapers. She heard him conversing with an even older European-born Jew.

"Hey, do you know," the newspaper vendor said, "that a hundred years ago there was no *El* here? A hundred years ago, McDonald Avenue was a bright street. There were rows of trees and freshly painted benches. In those days, my friend, Brooklyn was Brooklyn!"

"Listen," the Jew said hesitantly, "we believe in the Messiah. When the Messiah comes, McDonald Avenue won't be 'under the rails.' The Messiah will tear out the metal columns and the rails, put an end to the vibrations, and make it bright again here during the day."

"So, when will he come?"

"He'll come when he comes."

Not sure what to say, the newspaper vendor responded with the words from an old American folk-song: "*She'll be comin' 'round the mountain when she comes.*"

B.

Lenore walked the five minutes to her house, briefcase in hand. She was of medium height, had medium-length brown hair, freckles, horn-rimmed glasses, skinny hips, and a modest bosom. She didn't look any different from many

American Jewish girls – the only thing was that her lips were a little too thin for her face. From the way she was dressed, she appeared to be a Modern Orthodox girl: her dress was longer and looser than that of nonreligious or Gentile girls and shorter and tighter than that of the *khasidim* and the ultra-Orthodox. It was her last semester at college – in a few months she would have her diploma in philosophy. To her applications for jobs, there was, so far, one 'yes': an offer to become an assistant teacher in a high school somewhere far away in Canada. But what was the use of thinking about that now? She had to get through her exams successfully, and then she could talk.

Her home was a detached house with false bricks over the wooden outer walls, a small garden in front, and a yard in back. When she entered the kitchen, her parents had supper waiting. Robert was the manager of a Brooklyn bookkeeping firm; Karen was a math teacher in an elementary school.

"Good evening, Lenore. What's new?" her father asked in the kind of English that the Modern Orthodox speak, meanwhile straightening out the hairpin in his knitted *kipa.**

"Fine, thank you. Two lectures and the seminar. And you?"

"Not bad – new clients, a firm of electronics merchants who want to arrange things so they pay less tax in the spring. But I warn all my clients: 'If you pay less now, you'll pay more later, one way or another.' That's Robert's Law I tell them."

---

* Knitted modern skullcap or yarmulke.

During the conversation, her mother puttered around in the kitchen, opening all kinds of tin cans with prepared foods. This was America, not where their parents came from – one only had to heat things up, and by God's miracle there was already supper on the table.

Sitting at the table, it dawned on Lenore for the first time that her life and her house and her parents were dull and boring. Wasted years! She looked at the yellow walls and thought: "Out!" She managed, without difficulty though, to carry on a normal supper conversation so her parents shouldn't notice that their daughter's thoughts were elsewhere. The television played throughout the meal, and they always went quiet during the first fifteen minutes of the evening news program with Dan Rather.

After supper Lenore went up to her room to study. Upstairs in the hall, she passed the closed door of the storage room, and for a moment a chill ran down her spine. When she was a child, her grandmother, Sonke, Karen's mother, had lived there. She was an old Lithuanian Jew with fat arms, bushy eyebrows, and a slightly masculine mouth. She never learned any English. In America, she had nothing to do. Lenore learned colloquial Yiddish from her as a child. Her grandmother seldom left her room – she was afraid something would happen to her. All day long she waited for her grandchild to knock on the door; meanwhile, she wrote letters to her husband and her parents who had long been in the other world. Sonke thought that only letters written in Yiddish reached Heaven; communication had to be in writing, because talking to dead people was like talking to the wall.

C.

Lenore recalled a conversation from long ago – a quite ordinary one – between her grandmother and herself. Her grandmother used to call her Tsipke.

"Tsipke, come in! Why are you standing out here? Know that it is your grandmother Sonke who is speaking to you. I'm your grandmother, and I was born in the wonderfully beautiful city of Ignalina, in Lithuania – the most beautiful city on God's earth. Today we'd call it a small town, but to us Ignalina was not a small town but a city! Not just a city but a city with five beautiful lakes! Here in America, there are no such lakes. I'll name you the five lakes: Green Lake, Jewish Lake, Long Lake, Lake Gavaitis, and Lake Petrova. All around there were dense forests. *Sonke the eyebrow* they called me as a girl – even as a little girl I had bushy eyebrows. Tell me everything that happened to you today, Tsipke!"

"I quarrelled with my girl-friend."

"Tsipke, sit down here. We have to discuss this, and then we'll decide what to do."

"We were supposed to go ice-skating in the rink, but she went off with another girl. She didn't even leave me a note. I waited in the street for two hours, in vain."

"Look at me Tspike. Remember that you were named after my sister Tsipe-Leah. They called her Tsipke – if someone had yelled 'Lenore' in the street in Ignalina, she wouldn't have turned around. So, America, Shmerika, to me you're Tsipke. But I digress. Are you paying attention?"

"I'm listening, grandma. So?"

"Do what I do. Are you listening? Lick your lips with your tongue, around and around. Now say together with me:

'That's the end of the story – she's no longer my friend and the Devil with her!' You'll find a better one. Don't let her see that you're angry – say 'good morning' and 'good-year' and walk by. You're my grandchild, after all! And that's nothing to sneeze at: Sonke's grandchild!"

"Grandma! What you say is right! Grandma – do you believe in demons?"

"There's nothing to 'believe in.' I remember a demon in Ignalina very well, as if he were standing here in this room. His name was Maladreypke for short; his full name was Maladreype-Darvush. He lived on the mountains where the Ignalina cemetery was located, but a demon is not allowed to live in a holy place, so he lived on the other side of the mountain. We often went to the cemetery to visit the dead, to invite them for a holiday or a wedding."

"So why aren't there any demons in America?"

"They're not interested in anything here."

"What does 'Ignalina' mean?"

"Ah – good that you ask. A Gentile prince, Ignatz, fell in love with a Jewish girl, Lina (her Jewish name was Leahnyu.) He converted to Judaism and together they built the city, and Jews and Gentiles lived there together in peace for hundreds of years. That's the story they told us."

Once a month, Sonke used to take Lenore to New York (as Brooklynites invariably called Manhattan). Lenore liked it that her grandmother was enthusiastic about three things in the city: the escalators in Macy's department store, the lights that shone from under the sidewalk, and the steam that shot up to the sky from the middle of the street, as if to celebrate life with an eternal shower of silver-white fireworks from below.

On Sabbath, Lenore would sit next to her grandmother in the synagogue. When everyone responded with a brief 'Amen', her grandmother Sonke savoured a long, drawn-out, Lithuanian-Ashkenazi 'O-o-o-meyn.' Lenore was thrilled by that.

When Lenore was twelve years old, her grandmother went to live in an old-people's home somewhere in Connecticut. They saw her only rarely. She was not the same Sonke. Instead of being the hopeful person who told story after story, she was no more than any other old lady in a home for the aged. Lenore didn't understand why her grandmother couldn't continue to live with them in Brooklyn. Her parents explained that it was good for her grandmother herself. She missed her grandmother, but a young American girl has plenty to keep her busy: her schoolwork, her friends, television, movies and the yearly trips of her Hebrew day-school to Israel. There she like Ein Gedi* the best.

When she was eighteen, in the very month she started college, right after *rosh hashone*, news came that her grandmother Sonke had died. Lenore wept bitterly at the funeral. Feelings of guilt plagued her all through her first year at college. Why did I let them send grandmother Sonke to the old-peoples' home to rot? Why didn't I go there every Sunday? Why? Why? She said *kadish* every day, as she had

* An oasis near the Dead Sea.

been taught in the day-school, but when it came to the 'Amen', it was her grandmother's 'O-o-o-meyn': otherwise her grandmother in Paradise wouldn't hear it. And that reminded her that she had to write a few words occasionally to her grandmother in Paradise, in accord with her statement that the dead can receive only letters, and, indeed, only letters written in Yiddish.

D.

The few months raced by. After Passover came the last exams. She received her diploma and that Saturday night fell into a deep depression. Every week after Sabbath, even in the late summer, she would go to the movies, to the theatre, or to a concert, always with a group of six, eight, or ten Modern Orthodox young people, as was the custom. Her parents worried that at the age of twenty-two there was not even a sign of a boyfriend.

She wasn't eager to have one. The weekend after graduation, no one stayed in the city, but she stayed with her parents. Everything seemed desolate and empty to her.

Late one Saturday night, after Sabbath, her parents went to the late show at the movies. They invited Lenore to come along, but she declined; she would stay home to read and watch television.

Suddenly, a strange plan occurred to her. For the first time she wouldn't just walk through her neighbourhood, Midwood, up to McDonald Avenue, and get on the elevated train – she would walk to the 'other side of the tracks.' She laughed to herself when she remembered that in stories about the towns in Middle America, the train-tracks were a border between rich and poor, white and black, old residents and new arrivals. Here in Brooklyn there were precisely such tracks – the El! The El above McDonald Avenue separated the territories of two tribes that had nothing to do with one another. On one side, in Midwood, the Jews were Modern Orthodox, with Hebrew day-schools and Young Israel of Flatbush*. On the other side, which Lenore had only driven through on the way to the ocean as a child, was Boro Park. There one found *Anshei Marmerosh, Yeshiva D'Munkatsh, Beys Medresh D'Satmar* and *Beys Bobov.*† Between the two worlds stood the steel barrier, the El with its noisy trains. On rainy days, showers of sparks rained down on both sides of the barrier to announce that, whatever happens, brother, remember that a border is a border.

The neighbourhood right on the other side of McDonald Avenue was not so great; a girl didn't walk there alone after dark – this was no-man's land. Lenore rode the few stops on the bus and got off in the very heart of Boro Park, on Thirteenth Avenue. Everyone knew it was almost the only neighbourhood in New York where your life was safe day and night. If a criminal tried anything, people would immediately yell *'khaptzim*‡ – 'catch him!' – and a hundred *khasidim* would rain blows on the mugger and take him to the police-station, or straight to the hospital, depending on how much of a beating he had received.

---

* A well-known Orthodox Jewish institution.
† Various ultra-Orthodox *khasidic* schools and synagogues.
‡ Khasidic dialect form of Yiddish words for "catch him."

When the Sabbath was over, it didn't take long before Thirteenth Avenue became packed, the streets full of *khasidim*. They spoke a Yiddish that was quite different from hers; to Lenore, it was strange but attractive. One heard *gitvokh** everywhere – a city converted to one big *m'lave malke*[†], not like the city she knew, which was a basically Gentile city that happened to have Jews, synagogues, and orthodox homes where people greeted each other after Sabbath with *shavua tov.*[‡] The air in Boro Park smelled of Sabbath perfume. She noticed that all the women had rear seams in their stockings, which she had seen only in old movies. What was the point of that? Probably they thought it was less exciting to men. Who knows? In those old movies, after all, they thought just the opposite.

E.

Along Thirteenth Avenue, all the cross-streets were exactly at a right angle, decreasing by one number per street. Lenore walked and walked in that strange land, from 54th Street to 46th Street. There, next to a store that sold newspapers in Yiddish, English, Hebrew, and Hungarian, she saw a beggar sitting on a wooden box right near the wall. On the box, in large letters, was a sign: 'Jaffa oranges'. The man yelled to her in English with a Yiddish accent: "Twenty-five cents, please; just a quarter." Lenore immediately took out the coin.

---

* Yiddish dialect for "A good week!"
† "Accompanying the Queen"; bidding the Sabbath goodbye (often with a dinner event after the Sabbath is over).
‡ Israeli Hebrew for "A Good Week!"

Her unhurried walk as she approached him and placed the coin slowly in his tin cup, hinted to him: Talk to me. He asked her in English whether she was from Boro Park, knowing full well that she wasn't, and she – to his astonishment – answered in Yiddish. It was the first time she had spoken Yiddish to anyone other than her grandmother. She didn't know the word *ir** so she asked the beggar:

†*"Fun vanit kumste?"*

"I'm from Plungyan. In the same business as my father and grandfather, for nine generations already."

"I don't understand."

"I'll explain it to you. Charity is a great *mitsve*‡, so my business is not for me but to help Jews do a *mitsve*. I don't accept money from Gentiles, and certainly not from bad people."

"My grandmother used to say that the prophet Elijah disguised himself as a beggar, and for that reason one must not pass a beggar by without giving."

"A wise woman, your grandmother. Is she still living?"

"No, she's been dead for a few years." Lenore bowed her head.

"Was she from here?"

"What?"

"Born in America?"

"No, from a little town – Ignalina. It's from her that I learned my little bit of Yiddish."

---

* The polite form of "you" used in speaking to anyone other than family, servants and social inferiors, very close friends and God.

† "Where do you come from," using the familiar "*du*", here contracted to "*te*".

‡ A good deed commanded by the Bible.

"It's not so bad, and you know what? We're *landslayt*.*
Plungyan is also in Lithuania. It's all the same for Jews: we're
both Litvaks, *misnagdim*,† the same to all these *khasidim*
here in Boro Park, or rather '*Kapore*-Park'.‡ I'm not from
Boro Park – I come here once a week, on Sabbath, for 'business', as you see.

"What do you do the rest of the week?"

"That's a big secret."

"Oh, excuse me. What's your name?"

"My name is Nokhem. And you?"

"Uh – my name? Lenore."

"Listen – I want you to become a client, a customer.
Come next week after Sabbath, on Saturday night. Good
week."

Lenore went home pleased with her brief conversation with
the Boro Park beggar. She thought about Nokhem. He didn't
look very clean and he was terribly ugly. Wisps of hair
sprouted on his irregularly shaven face. His abnormally
pudgy hands lay motionless on his knees.

She went home and went to bed. That night she dreamed
an erotic dream for the first time. She was on a tropical
island with exotic trees. In the middle of the island was a
waterfall like the one in Ein Gedi. Lying next to the

* People from the same place.
† *Non-khasidic*, often anti-*khasidic* Jews, usually from Lithuania, Belarus,
or northeastern Poland.
‡ A nearly untranslatable disparaging remark about the residents of
Boro Park; a *kapore* is usually a chicken to which one transfers one's sins
to get rid of them.

waterfall, looking up, was Nokhem. He was stark naked. She slowly washed him all over with water from the waterfall and large leaves, and with each splash from the miraculous oasis in the middle of the Biblical desert his deformities were slowly undone; he began to look nicer and nicer, younger and younger, on the way to being a handsome young guy. As she washed him, she joked with him.

"Here I've found some dirt from five years ago. And there, near your neck, it's as black as if you haven't washed for ten years. Oh, oh, oh! Do you know what I've found? Here's tar from before the war."

After that, she lay down on a flat stone covered with moss. The transformed, prince-like Nokhem began to undress her very gently without saying a word. He kissed every inch of her body slowly and passionately. They made love three times, each time longer and more beautifully than the time before. Finally, she lay on the stone, sleepy from pleasure. Gradually, her rhythmic breathing subsided. But then, strangely, it all became undone and Nokhem reverted to the Beggar of 46th Street.

On Sunday morning, Lenore woke in a sweat. She was filled with shame, like an innocent Yeshiva student who had had a nocturnal emission during sleep. She ran to take a bath and emptied and refilled it three times with fresh hot water. No one was in the house.

Lenore began to go to Boro Park every Saturday night after the Sabbath ended. She went there five times, gave Nokhem his quarter each time, and had a brief conversation with him, which was always interrupted when a new 'customer' arrived. The sixth week she couldn't get out of having to go with her parents to visit some very boring cousins out on Long Island.

F.

The seventh Sabbath night went differently. Nokhem asked for fifty cents, two quarters. For the first time, one of the supposedly immobile hands moved upward. Like a seasoned merchant, he took a little notebook out of his breast pocket, in which it was recorded that Lenore hadn't come the previous Sabbath night. Now she owed him two whole quarters. Lenore gave him the fifty cents right away and tried to hide from Nokhem her surprise that he kept books in which he wrote down the names of 'clients' who missed a week.

"How's business?" she asked him.

"Slowish," he answered.

This time, no other 'client' came for a while. She conversed longer with him. Her Yiddish flowed more easily.

When a new client finally came, a young *khosid*, Nokhem asked Lenore to wait. She moved away, stood near Nokhem with her back to the wall, and listened.

"Good week, Reb Nokhem. Here's your alms."

"How many times do I have to explain to you that I don't take charity – I help you do a *mitsve*. If I took up another business, I too would live in a beautiful house, like a decent person, like God in Bobruisk.*"

"Yes, that's what I meant."

---

* An idiom roughly equivalent to "in clover."

"Here's a new customer of mine who's here for the seventh week already – first class! Right over there."

"Who is that girl?"

"Her grandmother and I come from the same place."

"Litvaks, hah Nokhem?"

"They call us Litvaks – we are followers of the Vilna Gaon and Reb Khayim Volozhiner. There in Europe, if you developed a calling to be a rabbi, you were sent to Volozhin and not to Hotzeplotz or Yehupets."*

"You understand Yiddish?" the young *khosid* asked Lenore, looking at an imaginary midpoint on the wall between her and Nokhem, as if it were geometrically measured.

"Yes, from my grandmother, but not very well."

"Are you a Sabbath observer?" he asked, and the corners of his mouth, hidden by his beard, half smiled at her sharp American 'r'.

"Of course! There are religious Jews who are not *khasidim*!"

"No, no – of course! I was just asking. You're surely a student someplace, no?"

"I was. I've just graduated."

"Mazl tov – In what?"

"Philosophy."

"Philosophy? Congratulations! I attend a yeshiva not far from here."

---

* Hotzeplotz is a term for some fictional insignificant town, and Yehupets is a fictional wealthy city modelled after Kiev (in Sholem Aleichem's work).

After that, the young man spoke spontaneously. He blushed, but you couldn't see it in the night-time street-lamp light.

"Could I speak to you for a few minutes sometime? I'm interested in that – I mean philosophy. Who knows – maybe you've read a little Rambam and B'chai*, and I thought we could have a chat, that is, if you have time."

"I have time now. Perhaps we could go in somewhere on Thirteenth Avenue."

"That's a good idea, but no – that's not so simple here. Anyway, I have to run – they're waiting for me in the middle of -. But maybe we'll meet again."

Lenore rescued him.

"Tomorrow I'll be in New York. Maybe we can meet there?"

"Oh! A good idea! Smart girl! Nokhem, give me a piece of paper from your notebook and she'll write down exactly where and when," the *khosid* said, trying to smooth over his actions by bringing Nokhem into the whole affair.

Sunday morning, the *khosid* said his morning prayers with particular fervour. He asked God to forgive him for meeting a girl on a corner somewhere in New York. At the same time, he complained to the Lord of the Universe: why is it a sin for a yeshiva student and a girl who is a Sabbath observer to talk publicly about the story of Creation, about free will, personal providence and the Eternal? In his morning prayers, he paid special attention to the prayer *He who opens the eyes of the blind*, trying to convince himself that it also referred to

* Rambam refers to Maimonides, and B'chai refers to the philosopher Bahya.

spiritual blindness. Perhaps it would be clearer after talking with a lady philosopher. In *shmoyne esre** he *concentrated* on *khoyneyn hada'as*. In *rabonon kadish*, when he came to *All the disciples of their disciples* he thought about the verse *I have learned from all my teachers;* he was not lacking in associations of lines and random quotes. The Talmudic analogies began multiplying in his mind. But nothing helped – the victorious Evil Spirit was flushed with victory; what was the use of making up stories – today he was going to meet a pretty young girl, a worldly person, in New York.

Nokhem, for his part, saw his business expanding: "Soon you'll owe me a matchmaker's fee. For now, you both just have to put in a quarter and tomorrow will go well for you."

G.

The rendezvous was on the corner of Broadway and Nineteenth Street in New York, at two o'clock. That's what was written in Lenore's handwriting on the beggar's piece of paper, which the young man had taken out of his pocket and looked at maybe a hundred times, as if there were hidden holy letters with the deepest secrets on the paper.

He left his house with unusually hopeful steps. Walking to the subway faster than usual, he was careful not to bump into the baby carriages with which the Boro Park streets were full on Sunday. Women showed off their pretty infants in the streets all day. In the half-empty subway car, the young man recited a 'subway psalm' from one of those tiny pocket editions of Psalms perfect for avoiding wasting time, or even

* A Jewish prayer.

worse, looking at some Gentile girl that the Devil, from time immemorial, working in concert with the Evil Inclination, had made a habit of seating right opposite. On Sundays, the trains crawled like tortoises. He started with a tremulous *ashrei ho'ish* from the start of the Book of Psalms and reached the 54th Psalm: '*To the choirmaster with stringed instruments: a song of David.*'

He got off at the Union Square station and walked the few blocks.

Even before the scheduled time, he was standing on the corner of Nineteenth Street and Broadway, clumsily leaning against a lamppost. His too-large trousers sagged behind him. There were spots on his white shirt. His sparse reddish beard flew in all directions. He looked at his little psalm again and bent back in prayer, but this time it was pure make-believe. Passersby looked to see why the *khosid* was standing there; usually they saw *khasidim* only during the week, during work-hours, and they were always running somewhere to some office high up in some building where they were engaged in God-knows-what kind of business.

H.

Suddenly Lenore appeared. She smiled broadly. The young man blushed; his face and his reddish beard became a single red entity. His blue eyes looked like two lakes in a parched desert land.*

---

* The conversation that follows has mildly amusing verbal word play in the original Yiddish, based on dialect differences between Litvaks and *khasidim*. Since that word play is untranslatable, the conversation has been presented straightforwardly.

"I've come without even knowing your name," she began.

"My name is Heshi. And you*?"

"Lenore. In Hebrew, it's Tsipora. But my grandmother used to call me Tsipke, after her sister Tsipe-Leah."

"Let it be Lenore. So, are we going to stand here and talk?"

"No. There's a kosher restaurant not far from here – that's why I chose this corner."

"Good choice! But no – they'll look at me as if it were *purim*†. The Modern Orthodox will look at us in complete bafflement. Let's go to an ordinary restaurant instead. I hope you've brought a paper cup with you. I'm sure they'll agree to pour some Jewish whisky into it – they'll charge for the whisky, and here in Manhattan they're used to everything anyway."

"What does 'Jewish whisky' mean?"

"Black coffee – that's something a Jew can drink anywhere."

"It's a strange world – a *khosid* can go into a Gentile restaurant but not into a kosher one!"

"OK, let's go!"

I.

Walking together on Twentieth Street, they didn't say a word. They looked for an ordinary little diner or cafe on one of the wide avenues farther on. They passed several cafes that were too small – they wouldn't have felt sufficiently

* Here Heshi uses the polite "ir."
† A Jewish holiday when people often dress up in costumes.

anonymous there. Two homeless men wrapped in rags were lying on the sidewalk next to the entrance to a closed store; the odour there was far from perfume. Farther on, in a side-alley, a hobo was urinating. A fancily dressed prostitute couldn't restrain herself and jokingly yelled to the *khosid* that he should take the girl home and then come back, but right away.

Finally, they found a cafeteria with a narrow vestibule where patrons gathered to pay, and in the back a large room with little tables. For the first half hour, the conversation was stiff and awkward, but amid the black, white, brown, and oriental customers they relaxed and realized that no one cared that they were sitting at a little table with cups of coffee – she with the restaurant's cup, he with his black garments, red side-curls, and the paper cup he had brought along. They joked that with such a cup a holy and pious Jew could travel the world; in fact, vodka and whisky were deemed to be equally kosher.

Lenore told Heshi about Socrates, Plato, and Aristotle, and then turned to her specialty, the British empiricists Locke, Berkeley, and Hume. She told him about those things in Yiddish mixed with a lot of English terms. He was not intimidated and said that Rabeynu B'Chai had summarized them all in one sentence: "If you throw a bottle of ink on the ground, it won't turn into a book", and in the same way, the world was not created without God. Lenore answered that she agreed because of her faith, but not because that made sense. David Hume, after all, demonstrated that everything that people considered logic is nothing more than experi-ence. The mind abstracts principles from that which the senses have absorbed; you see that if you drop something, it falls down and not up, and that becomes a principle, not noticing that it's all just experience. That's the case with B'Chai's arguments, too (she called him Bakhya, not by his Yiddishized name); one can't deduce from what happens in front of the one's eyes what happened at a time before there were people with eyes.

After that, they got down to brass tracks. Both of them were happy for the first time, being close to one another. Both trembled from the force that had come to tell them that this wasn't just one more day in God's world and had said: "This is it – go no farther." It didn't occur to the two people in the cafeteria that they needed to make additional dates to find out whether they were suited to one another, whether they liked the same movies. Not a single word of love or affection, or even praise, passed between them, but they both knew they didn't want to part. Without any preliminaries, they started to talk about what was going to happen. Heshi looked at his watch. He'd soon have to run so he wouldn't miss afternoon prayers. That was a signal that they had to decide on something. Lenore said that she had been offered a job somewhere far away in Canada. Heshi answered that he was soon going to go to the Catskills for the summer. His yeshiva ran a summer camp there, not far from Mountaindale, New York. She then said that it was not so far from there to Poughkeepsie, where there was a train station on the Canada line.

"I can't just go that easily. I have parents, grandparents, sisters, and brothers that I love very much. To them, someone like you would be considered simply a catastrophe."

"I'm not a *shikse*, and I observe Sabbath. Is it all because I'm not a *khosid*? What's all that about? I'll even give some credence to Bakhya's interpretation."

"I can assure you that your parents will have exactly the same reaction. Or even worse!"

"No, they're tolerant, modern people."

"So, by all means talk to them and you'll see for yourself, and let's meet here next Sunday at exactly two o'clock."

"Don't forget the paper cup."

J.

Heshi approached the matter somewhat abstractly. He asked his father's opinion about a Modern Orthodox girl who has never in her life desecrated Sabbath, even speaks Yiddish, though a bit strangely, is definitely a virgin, and graduated college with a degree in philosophy.

"I'm sure you're not just asking – okay, so where did you meet such a girl, tell me?"

"What difference does it make?"

"You said the words, not I. Any girl who has gone to college is not going to be faithful to her husband, and that's putting it nicely. There have been cases where, in the end, some ostensibly became penitents, practically saints, and went to the hospital to be sewn up. Became real virgins!"

"You can't talk that way about all of them, Daddy, because some may be really pious. In fact, a lot of them are."

"Maybe, but not for my son! Let's rather start to look for a respectable match – maybe now you won't say 'she's no good' about anyone that someone mentions to you."

From the summer camp in the mountains, he sent his father a letter telling him that he was going to Canada 'for a while'. He felt certain that his father would forgive him in the end and that everything would be all right.

K.

At supper that Sunday, Lenore told her parents that she had met a fine young man. They hadn't felt such joy in all her twenty-two years. Their English grew rapid, with a special Yiddishy intonation that appeared only when they got visibly excited.

"A medical doctor, maybe, or a lawyer?" Robert, a born optimist, asked.

"No!" Karen corrected him. "Lenore will choose a philosopher or a sociologist, or even a historian. Yes, Lenore?"

"He's actually . . ." And then, after a long and seemingly endless pause, "a *khosid,* a yeshiva student in Boro Park. He speaks English poorly, so I speak to him in Bubby's Yiddish."

Her parents both turned pale. Their forks fell with a loud crash onto the yellow oilcloth on the table. Finally, Robert, who couldn't conceal his disgust, started asking her questions.

"Is he dirty like all of them?"

"I'll clean him up!" Lenore said, and immediately felt heartsick for having agreed that *khasidim* were 'dirty'.

"I think Lenore should go to Israel again this summer. I'll pay for it."

"No, thank you, Mama. I'm going to accept the job offer in Canada, and I'll be settling there right away. Maybe Heshi will come too."

"Heshi?" she grimaced. "What's his real name?"

"That's his name."

Lying in bed that night, Lenore overheard, through the thin walls, the entire quarrel between her parents:

"It's all your fault! If your mother hadn't lived here in the house for all those years, our daughter would have grown up normal. Who ever heard of a grandmother living in the house!"

"How dare you bad-mouth my mother? She lived through such terrible things! She never said a bad word to you. And besides, you insisted that we send her to that desolate old-people's home, where she languished like a dog in her last years."

"It's a lie! It was the best old-age home in Connecticut. I paid a fortune so she could get in there. I had to use all my connections."

"So, what will people say if our freshly graduated daughter goes away with a *khosid* from Boro Park whose name is Heshi?"

"She'll come around to common sense and reason; young people have to have their adventures. Remember, this could be much worse – think about what happened to the Bernsteins . . ."

"It's no use. She was never interested in any young man, so if she's talking about a young man now and is going to Canada in any case, it's all over."

"Shh . . . Lenore can probably hear everything we're saying."

Lying in bed, Lenore wept silently; she didn't even bother to wipe her eyes. She thought about her grandmother, Sonke, how much she had loved her, how she had forgotten about her when she went away to rot in the old-people's home. Now she was rotting even more in a disgusting American cemetery, where, at the entrance, there was a complicated list of the hours when the cemetery was open during the week and on Sundays, legal holidays, and Jewish holidays. During office hours they sold overpriced books about Jewish mourning traditions. No homey demon would be interested in looking in over there. When her eyes dried a bit, she saw a streak of light on the ceiling, a diagonal representation of the opening between the curtains. Right in the streak of light there was a spider. At first, Lenore felt disgusted, but then she began to study the spider and its long shadow. She admired how the spider didn't fall, how six of its legs were symmetrically spread out while the other two were stretched out in front of it.

L.

On the Sabbath night before leaving – Heshi was at the summer camp, and they already knew on which train they would meet the following day – Lenore went to Boro Park to see Nokhem. She didn't tell him anything. She gave him an envelope containing thirty-nine single dollars – what she owed him for the next three years, paid in advance. Nokhem barely raised his hand. He asked her to put the sealed envelope into his breast pocket. Oh, she thought to herself, what she wouldn't give to see his expression when he opened the envelope!

The following day, she got on the train in Grand Central Station in New York. When the train stopped in Poughkeepsie, Lenore poked her head out the window and shouted:

"Heshi! Here!"

He got into the railroad car and the train immediately started up again. Sitting there, they were two eternal lovers between whom there had never been a word of love, let alone a kiss. To both of them, the most beautiful word in the world was 'Canada'. The train, traveling northward, passed by fields, farms, towns, and forests. Brooklyn, where two families on either side of McDonald Avenue were each mourning a child, receded farther and farther behind them.

The Jewish Christmas

A.

The modern cuckoo clock sounded three times.

"Well, Mort. It's already past 3 o'clock! So where are they, your very dear relatives that you can't live without?" his wife Felicia said harshly.

Morton looked a lot younger than his sixty-two years. He was unusually handsome, with a youthful body and a thick head of snow-white hair. Morton was no more and no less than the American dream: forty years earlier, he had gotten a job as an errand boy for a big brokerage firm on the Wall Street Stock Exchange, had gradually worked himself up, and had finally become president of the firm. Every morning he went jogging. But for all his American-ness, he liked to speak Yiddish and to get together with those of his relatives who had remained in the city, especially his eldest brother, Osip.

Felicia had no choice – she had to receive everyone. That's what Morton wanted. That was all there was to it. She herself was chubby and came from a poor Jewish family in the Bronx. She coloured her hair to a colour between muddy brown and shining silver. She constantly had a cold – wherever Felicia was, there was a handkerchief.

"They'll come soon. What do a few more minutes matter?" Morton soothed her. He was pleased that Osip, his eldest brother, was coming soon; he was the only one in the family who had remained a 'European Jew'. With him one could have a drink of whisky and a good time, like in the old days. Osip had studied in a yeshiva in Europe. He was a composer and also a teacher of Jewish music, about which he had published books. He played the old-time tunes beautifully on the violin.

Felicia could tolerate Osip, and even his wife Rokhl, an artist, but she couldn't stand Osip's son, Aaron, a sort of professor of philosophy somewhere in Canada, who spoke both too loudly and too sharply and vulgarly for her ears, and in addition with a lisping Brooklyn accent. Today not only were Osip, Rokhl, and Aaron supposed to come, but also two of Aaron's friends. If Aaron was bringing them, what in the world could they be like?

In addition, Dorothy, Morton's tragic elder sister, was also supposed to be coming. Felicia and Morton constantly quarrelled with her, bitter quarrels with the most terrible words. Aaron's worst trait in Felicia's eyes was that he remained close to Dorothy (he called her by her Jewish name: Dvosye.) Felicia would ask who had ever heard of such a thing – that a young man should go visit his old aunt and take her side in the family fights. Once Felicia and Morton had specially invited Aaron alone, when he was still a student in New York, and had tried to convince him that Dorothy was a nuisance who would be an emotional parasite on him in his adult life if he wasn't forewarned. The young man, however, stubbornly insisted that he loved Dorothy and had pity on the old, lonely women who had had nobody since her husband, an athlete who was as healthy as an ox, had suddenly died in the fullness of youth, who knows how many years ago.

But there was one consolation for Felicia today – two real Americans were supposed to come from Connecticut: Morton's nephew Teddy and his wife, Lettie. They got along with everybody and didn't get involved in quarrels. Normal people.

That afternoon was Christmas, the great Christian holiday that begins on the eve of December 25th. Some Jews call it, in Yiddish, '*nitl*'. To most American Jews, it is plain 'Christmas'. Though Morton and Felicia were Jews, and didn't celebrate Christmas, inviting the family on precisely that day couldn't hurt, they thought. Just the opposite – common sense said that that's what you should do. For one thing, everyone is free from work that day. The non-Jews all get together and rejoice about what the world stands on, and where is it written that Jews should sit alone and weep? Most Gentiles have a Christmas tree, but whom should it bother if Jews gather without such a tree? With a tree, without a tree – sitting alone when it's holiday time everywhere is not the way to go.

The Kahanovs were waiting.

At home, Morton trembled before Felicia; that was because at work he had lovers – you shouldn't speak about them – young women with short dresses and broad smiles. He liked exotic girls; Korean, Indonesian, African. Most of all he liked his Chinese secretary, whom he called 'Ti' for short. Ti was not a young girl with a short skirt – she was his age, an unusually refined, quiet women in whose presence it was a pleasure to be.

There was a certain understanding between husband and wife: he did whatever he wanted at work, but at home she was the boss. He had assured his wife that as soon as the guests came he would scold them for being late. Felicia had a short hairdo that didn't suit her, least of all in tandem with its weird colouring; the Chinese secretary had the same hairdo but it did suit her, and with her hair coloured black, it seemed not to matter at all.

The large, rich house stood in a town called Massapequa, in Long Island, not very far from Manhasset. No matter how big the house was, after they built it it wasn't big enough. The house grew. Every couple of years, Felicia would run to the architects anew and sit for days with the 'designers' and the planners about where and how to add to the house: below the cellar, another cellar: above the roof, another storey; and most of all they built 'extensions' so the lowest floor grew wider. The more successful Morton was at work, the more rooms Felicia added to the Long Island palace out in Massapequa.

But you shouldn't think that Felicia built all that just to show off her wealth – that would have been a waste of money. One had to build with good sense and understanding. Through building additions, one gives every room a purpose and no void remains. One creates separate sections of the house for all kinds of guests. Thus, the beautiful original parlour with the brick chimney and the thick purple drapes would be left for important guests, distinguished people, and very wealthy people from Wall Street, sometimes even a politician. How would it look for the boorish louts from Morton's family to come in and wreck that room? So, they added a small room on the other side of the chimney, with two entrances, one on either side of the hearth. A chimney that can be seen from only one side, after all, is something everyone has, but this was a chimney around which one could make circular processions, as the religious Jews do around the Scrolls of the Torah on the *simkhas torah* holiday. In the little room on the other side of the chimney, there was a black leather sofa that had been imported from Kenya. That was the place into which one could bring important guests for a moment and speak to them. It should probably be called 'behind the oven' American-style.

The elegant dining-room was for middle-status guests.

In the cellar rooms – the 'basement', that is – they received intimate friends from Massapequa itself. There were ping-pong tables, various exercise machines, and an underground miniature golf course. All the basement additions extended far enough beyond the original foundations for there to be little transom windows on the perimeters. And that meant the addition of Doric columns for support, well, made to look Doric to give the basement the same aura of grandeur as the rest of the house.

They had built a big extension especially for Morton's family (Felicia, to be fair, didn't allow her own family to come anywhere near the house – they had to be entertained in Queens restaurants). Together with the designers and the planners, Felicia had thought of everything: the walls were brick, so the relatives couldn't dirty the painted walls; the table was made of glass, so the relatives seated there should tremble lest they break it; from the ceiling, a complicated chandelier hung very low, so they should worry about banging their head on it, or even worse, damaging the hundreds of *tshatshkes* that hung from it. Behind the table near the wall, there was a single lacquered wooden shelf that projected from the wall; there Felicia had set out little boxes containing knick-knacks, mostly porcelain eggs, and also archaeological antiques from Israel, with paper certificates of authenticity unaesthetically dangling from each. If one wasn't a ballet dancer, it wasn't that easy to manoeuvre between the table and the shelf – one could get poked in the ribs or would be afraid of breaking the expensive trinkets that were standing there, set out as if they were yelling:

"Silly – why are you silent? Break something!"

Even more important than the room itself, however, was its location in the house. One could enter and leave the family room only through the kitchen. They had built a new door that led to the outside from the side of the house, near the garages (there had once been two garages, but one of them had been sacrificed in order to build the extension for Morton's relatives). It was a sign that guests had to come in through the side of the house. On a day when they were being expected, if someone knocked on the front door, no one would pay any attention to the knock.

B.

At a quarter after three, there was a knock on the kitchen door. Felicia yelled:

"It's open! Why are you knocking?"

The first ones to come in were the elder brother, Osip, his wife, Rokhl, and his son, Aaron, who had driven down from Canada. Osip, who was in his seventies, had a young and energetic bearing. He gave his brother a warm handshake.

"Meylekh, how are you? It's wonderful to see you! Give me your hand! Felicia, how are you?"

Osip couldn't bring the name 'Morton' to his lips. Meylekh! Felicia had to give Osip a kiss, which was not easy for her. Osip was really very happy that the family was meeting. Despite the many years since the family had left their *shtetl* right after the First World War, they were holding together. Of the original brothers and sisters, only Morton, the youngest, had been born in America.

Osip and his family together formed a sort of caricature: as much as the no-longer young Osip was young, slender, quick-moving, and of medium height, his wife was short and fat and his son was tall and fat. Looking at them, one could immediately tell that the man was jolly, the wife was nervous, and the son was a nervous person who made himself out to be jolly, but it didn't help. Aaron always tried to make everyone jolly, to amuse the crowd. He indeed acted jolly, but everyone saw that his jolliness was artificial – he was his mother's child who wanted to be his father's child.

With them in the car had also come Morton's sister, Dorothy. Aaron had insisted on making a special trip to Manhattan to get her. Felicia resented that – she liked to have it that everyone should come by auto and Dorothy should have to come by train. Dorothy, already in her seventies (she was only two years younger than Osip), was very slender. Her face had become old, but her body was that of a young girl. In the street, young men, when they saw her from behind, thought that she was a young beauty. She wore stiff black trousers, a stiff black blouse, and a lot of rouge. Her dyed black hair was trimmed short. Morton said to Osip quietly:

"Just look at Dvosye! She looks like a black spider! I could vomit!"

"Well, it's wonderful when we all get together."

Osip avoided anything that could lead to a quarrel. Dorothy was looking at them bitterly from the other side of the kitchen. She couldn't hear them, but she *knew* they were laughing at her.

Felicia didn't say hello to Dorothy, but asked grumpily:

"Why didn't you tell me you were coming with them? I called the railroad station specially to find out about your usual train!"

"Why should I come by train when Aaron would come to get me?"

It took a few minutes till they noticed that there were two strange guests. Those were the two young Christians, both English, from London, that Aaron had met in the college in Canada in which he taught. Amelia was Aaron's girlfriend; she had come to make the acquaintance of the family for the first time. The other one, Cliff, was a former student of Aaron's. Both of them had nowhere to go this Christmas in a foreign land. Both of them had assured Aaron over and over that not only did they not resent not spending their time with Christians who were celebrating Christmas properly, but just the opposite – it would be a novelty for them to spend it with Jewish friends for the first time.

Everyone started to talk to the two non-Jews – they immediately grilled them: Who are you? How old are you? How are things there in Canada? Why did you move from England to Canada? Is this the first time you've been to Massapequa? The first time to New York?

In the room, one could feel the hatred between Morton's wife, Felicia, and his sister Dorothy. They had been at daggers drawn for forty years – one could even say it was from the first moment they had seen each other. Felicia felt that Dorothy wanted Morton to spend more time with her, as her husband had before he died; Morton had in fact been an angel to her in the years following her young husband's sudden death all those years ago. Dorothy had never remarried. Felicia told everyone that Dorothy was crazy and wanted only to provoke quarrels. Dorothy, however, was not one of those weak little widows who are so easily frightened. She blamed Felicia for being unable to forgive the fact that Morton had remained close to her, Dorothy. She told everyone that Felicia had 'grabbed' Morton when he was young and naive, and that he had married her because she lived nearer to him than his other girlfriends, and that right after their marriage she had forced him to move away far from his parents. It hadn't suited her, Miss America, to spend time with his greenhorn parents (Felicia duly kept her own greenhorn parents to compartmentalized monthly meetings in a Queens deli).

Both Felicia and Dorothy wanted to live to see only one thing: that the other one should have a stroke and lie sick and helpless in a hospital or an old-age home, and she would come visit her with false sympathy and beautiful presents. Then it would be clear who was the winner and who was the loser. Till then it was – war.

Everyone was standing in the kitchen. Dorothy asked loudly:

"Why are we all standing in the kitchen? Let's sit down at the table."

"No – we're waiting for Teddy and Lettie," Felicia answered her. Both of them looked at the ceiling when they spoke to one another. Dorothy immediately shot back:

"Who needs them? They're not real family!"

"I'll invite whoever I please to my house. It's time that you invite someone to your place – after all, you live in a beautiful apartment in the middle of Manhattan. When *you* make an invitation, you can invite whoever *you* please."

"Oh, please! You don't know what you're talking about! How can I invite anyone? I live all alone. You'll never understand what I suffer day in and day out. The loneliness! Thank God you haven't had to experience such terrible loneliness! Whom would I invite? Why is it so hot here? You could die from the heat! I can't breathe. Let's open a window."

Dorothy's nephew Aaron took her side and meanwhile tried to make things jolly:

"It is indeed terribly hot. But why open a window? There's a big, beautiful air-conditioner standing here – just a minute, I'll turn it on."

"Don't touch that!" Felicia yelled. "It's turned off for the winter and covered on the outside. Everything he has to break!"

"Crazy people!" Morton interrupted, with a friendly satirical tone, addressing his brother in Yiddish. "It's four below zero outside – four below zero! They said on the radio today that this is the coldest Christmas in sixty years. So, people come to a house and complain that it's too hot! Osip, have you ever in your life ever heard such a thing?"

Osip wasn't taking any chances. "Well – it's wonderful that we all come together and have a good time. Why do we need to talk – let's have a drink. *Lekhayim*, Meylekh! *Lekhayim*, Felicia! *Lekhayim*, Dvosye! *Lekhayim*, Rokhl! *Lekhayim*, Aaron! *Lekhayim*, Amelia! and *lekhayim*, Cliff! Everyone has to clink glasses – all together: *Lekhayim!*"

Suddenly, the last guests, Teddy and Lettie from Connecticut, appeared in the kitchen. Felicia called the guests to the great glass table in the 'extension' and showed everyone where to sit. Dorothy complained that Felicia had given her a chair with a crooked seat that would hurt her back. Felicia began bringing out of the oven the dishes that had been bought earlier from the big Jewish delicatessen in town. Osip, the eldest, sat at the head of the table. At his left sat his sister Dorothy, and on his right sat the Wall Street executive Morton, who was, today, Meylekh, enjoying his brother and the old-country humour that lived on.

C.

They began to eat, and things got jolly. The brothers Osip and Morton, their sister Dorothy, and Osip's son, Aaron, drank whisky. The mistress of the house, Felicia, Osip's wife Rokhl, and the two cousins from Connecticut, Teddy and Lettie, drank orange juice. The two young English guests drank beer – Morton had brought them six cans of Irish beer from the refrigerator.

Teddy looked at Aaron, who looked a lot older than his twenty-seven years, with his gigantic belly, his fat face, his sparse teeth, and his more-than-half-grey hair, which, in addition, was beginning to fall out in an unusual pattern. Good-humouredly, he asked:

"Aaron – there's one thing I'd like to know. Where do you come to a girl as pretty as Amelia? What does she see in you? Where did you find her?"

Aaron took a great deal of pleasure from their giving him an opportunity to have fun, and immediately began to chatter away loudly, as if he were waxing ecstatic about his own cleverness.

"It was like this. For three months I didn't have a girl-friend, so I put an ad in our local newspaper near the university. What kind of ad? OK. The ad said: 'Fat, neurotic, Brooklyn-born Jewish guy whose grey hair is falling out is looking for a beautiful *shikse*, to teach her genuine Jewish culture.' What happened? They came to me from all around. I interviewed each girl, and I chose this lucky Amelia. That's the way it was, Amelia, yes or no?"

"Don't talk so loud," Felicia yelled. "You don't have to give us all a headache."

Amelia blushed for a moment. She had already had a couple of glasses of beer, and she too wanted to have a little fun.

"I came along and immediately corrected his note, saying he had to say "*shikste*", not "*shikse*". He chose me, and now here I am in New York."

The audience began to laugh, talking, chattering and having fun. Quietly, Amelia said to Aaron:

"See how nice it is here. I love all the Jewish humour – it reminds me of Woody Allen. Why did you tell me that there's always a quarrel when you come to your uncle's in Massapequa?"

Aaron gave her a sign with his finger that meant: 'Wait a minute.' When it got a little quieter, he asked loudly, looking straight ahead, as if a teacher in a classroom were asking nobody in particular and waiting for a first respondent:

"There's one thing I want to ask. Was the family rich or poor in Europe?"

It was as if someone had lobbed a bomb through the window. Osip was the first to answer:

"I remember – after all, I'm older than everyone here. We were dying from hunger during the First World War, and even when there were good times, we had only potatoes. Ours was a little, poor *shtetl*. Our little house had an earthen floor."

Dorothy grew immediately crazy with anger:

"Oh stop! I can't bear it when you tell lies! My grandfather – Osip called him Nosson-Velvl, but his business name was Wolf Rappaport – was very rich. He had a big business exporting wood. Everyone knew him as the rich man of the *shtetl*."

Osip and Morton began to laugh. Morton spoke up:

"Oh sure! He was Rothschild! That's why we were so rich in Passaic, New Jersey, when we came here. Oh sure!"

"Stop it," Dorothy barked. "Of course they were poor in Passaic during the Depression, like everyone else. But back in Europe?"

Osip was afraid of a quarrel, so he immediately had a plan:

"Now I'll play a song on the violin. It's an old Jewish tune for dancing."

He began to play and it grew quiet again. But, right in the middle of his playing, Dorothy started to talk to him quietly.

"Why aren't Morton's children here today? They have contempt for the family! Their eldest son has already married a disgusting *shikse,* and they've tried to correct that by buying a piece of paper from the great rabbi from some other town called Manhasset that says she has converted to a Jew! It should happen to my enemies what kind of Jew she's become and what kind of rabbi he is in Manhasset! The other two sons will grab bitches like their mother or just plain *shikses.* You'll see whether I'm right! That's how she brought them up, that Felicia. Morton trembles before her. He won't say a word. That's why he is silent when she attacks me right in front of everybody. He's become just like his wife. Our mother used to say: "If you sleep long enough with a goye you become like the *goye.*" Osip put down his violin. He was sure that now it would be quiet. He didn't know that Morton had heard everything Dorothy had said to him while he was playing. With murder in his eyes, Morton, the usually staid Wall Street guy in the family, got up. Everyone was astonished.

"I heard every word you said to Osip there in the corner!"

"Osip, did I say anything?" Dorothy dragged Osip into the matter.

"No-o," Osip answered, hoping that with a pleasant 'No' he would avoid a quarrel. Morton continued to speak standing up.

"The whole of disgusting stuff I hear from your mouth reeks of gall. I'm sixty-two years old, and you are a hell of a lot older than me, so don't deny it. I'm too old for all this. You come here not as a friend – you come and sit and say out loud the most ugly things against me, against my wife Felicia, against my sons. What bad thing did we do to you? If we are such bad people, don't come! Who needs to have you here? And today is not the first time. Two weeks ago, when Osip was here, I accidentally picked up the new telephone extension upstairs and I heard everything you said against me and about Felicia. But when you need something, who do you go to? You go to Felicia! Then she's all right! When you were sick and you wanted someone to take you to the hospital, who did you ask? Felicia! When you need something, she's good. If you don't like it here, don't come!"

Morton sat down quietly, as if he had just given a speech at the United Nations. Everyone sat dumbstruck, shocked. Suddenly Dorothy got up and pointed at Felicia.

"May I drop dead this minute if I ever asked Felicia to take me to the hospital! Felicia called me and suggested that she take me. Let her deny that! If I am lying, may I drop dead this minute!"

Amelia, the Londoner, who had been astonished by all this, could not understand why a quarrel was revolving around the question of who was rich or poor back in the old country or, indeed, whether Dorothy had asked Felicia to take her or Felicia had suggested it.

"But what difference does it make?" she asked.

The second young Englishman, Cliff, was already drunk from the beer. He rapped on a glass three times with a spoon and then said:

"Ding, ding, ding – end of round two."

D.

Everyone stood up for a few minutes to catch their breath. Rokhl helped Felicia remove the old dishes and bring new ones. Whoever needed to, went to the special bathroom that had been built next to the kitchen for the relatives who were using the 'extension'. Felicia yelled that they should go back to the table – if not, everything would get cold.

When they had begun eating again, Lettie from Connecticut opened her mouth for the first time. She was a pretty woman who had preserved her youthful appearance extraordinarily well.

"Dorothy, I want you to know that I understand you very well. I have a brother, and I know what kind of problems can develop. But you must remember one thing – that Meylik and Felicia hold the family together. Who else would invite everyone the way they do?" she asked Dorothy quietly. Since Osip was in the room, by calling Morton 'Meylekh' she wanted to show off that she was indeed a Jewish girl, even if 'Meylik' was as close as she could manage out in Connecticut.

"Shut your mouth!" Dorothy yelled. "It's none of your business! Why are you getting involved? You're not even part of our family! You only married Teddy. And in addition to that, you're a fool! You don't know what you're talking about! You're stupid! You were always stupid!"

"Perhaps I am indeed a fool, but I do have a brother. For that reason, I think we could be friends and talk about all the problems. I believe in communication as a solution to all problems that occur between people."

"Shut your mouth! You're stupid!"

"Dorothy – don't you dare speak that way to a guest in my house! Do you hear me? Don't you dare!" Felicia interrupted.

"I'll say what I want, Felicia. You've hated me all your life. My mother wept because Morton married you. You're a cold fish without a crumb of humanity. A cold fish!"

Morton got up again and again started to speak.

"Look here, Dorothy – you hate Felicia, you hate Lettie. Do you know what the truth is? The truth is that you hate any woman who has a husband, you begrudge her that. You hate any women who is not an embittered old widow!"

"Just look at the way he attacks me! She incites him, that wife of his," Dorothy answered quickly, pointing at Felicia.

Osip started to feel sick to his stomach of all this. He gave his son a friendly kick under the table and whispered in his ear:

"Aaron! Be Kissinger! Let's see, by all means – show us a trick and make peace! Let's see if you can do that."

Aaron's friend Cliff, a young, intellectual British leftie, happened to hear this, and he too whispered in Aaron's ear:

"Tell your father that Kissinger is a mass murderer! Doesn't he know what Kissinger did in Vietnam? And in Cambodia?"

E.

Everyone stood up again for a few minutes. Felicia asked Rokhl to count how many wanted coffee and how many wanted tea. Aaron went up to his aunt Dorothy and had a plan for her:

"If you want, I'll drive you to Manhattan now. We'll go in somewhere to have a cup of coffee and enjoy ourselves far from everyone. What do you say?"

"Am I crazy? I'm not afraid of her! I'm staying right here!" And she got up to go out for a few minutes to fix her makeup. Her handbag, which she held in her right hand, pushed everything that was on the laminated shelf to the floor. Porcelain eggs, knick-knacks, and Israeli antiquarian treasures with their dangling authenticity certificates fell to the floor with a great clatter. A little plate from Bar Kochba's times broke into little pieces.

"Aw shit! My best pieces," Felicia cried out.

"Excuse me – I didn't see your trinkets standing there. I'll pay you for them."

"It's not a matter of money – you can't replace those things!"

A moment passed, and Dorothy sat down on a sofa in the corner. They hadn't yet called people to coffee. Osip's wife, Rokhl, went up to her and asked, out of pity, how she was doing. Dorothy didn't want pity.

"Why are you coming to talk to me when you always lick Felicia's behind!"

Rokhl, who had been sitting quietly all day, suddenly broke out into hysterics. The arteries on her forehead stood out. She began rhythmically jumping back and forth.

"I've heard enough from you about 'behind'. Behind, behind, behind. We don't hear anything else from you. You deserve everything you get from everyone! You deserve it! You've earned it all! You say only 'behind' to everyone! Behind, behind, behind! Only behind! Behind, behind, behind!"

Rokhl began to yell and to jump higher and higher. Felicia couldn't hide her pleasure. A broad smile appeared on her face. Today she was the winner. Dorothy had gotten it from everyone! Everyone hated her, hated her like a spider! Felicia had lived to see this day! Everyone hated Dorothy!

Suddenly, Amelia, seeing that Rokhl was hysterical, ran out of the room and began to cry. She had just spent a week as a guest in Rokhl's and Meylekh's house, as their son's girl-friend. She ran past the door leading to the bathroom and went into the first doorway after that. The room was painted entirely red – it was the 'Red Room', where unimportant overnight guests slept. Aaron immediately ran after her to see what was wrong.

"Excuse me, Aaron! Oy, I feel so bad about how I behaved in front of your family, that I ran out and started crying. I'm so sorry I got upset in front of your family. Excuse me!"

"Excuse *you*? What kind of nonsense is that? We are a band of nuts, and you say 'excuse me'! That's too funny! I'm going to tell them – at *that* they'll laugh, and that'll change their mood if anything will!"

In the kitchen they were already putting on their coats. Osip took out his violin again and played an extremely lively folk-dance.

It suddenly dawned on Morton that the two young British Gentile guests had seen everything. A small smile turned the corners of his mouth. He went up to Osip.

"Osip! I have to talk to you about a very important matter. Come into the other room for a minute. You know what? It's terrible! The English folks will think that Jews get together on precisely this day to curse Jesus, and since it's not nice to curse him directly, they create a great family quarrel and each one curses the others instead."

ENGLAND

A Day in Whitechapel

A.

Liza Thompson didn't overwork herself in her job in the great British Museum library in London. When people laid their request-card for books in the small open-topped oaken box, she took it and duly placed it in the hard rubber cylinder, closed it, and stuffed it into the mysterious tubes in which it travelled like an ancient little train on a children's planet, to the room of rooms in the deepest cellar where all the books lie hidden.

That summer, there was a heatwave in London. Hearing someone say to someone else: "Brother, it's hot! We can't go on this way!" Liza had thought: What a comedy! In the winter, day and night they vent their anger on the weather, complaining that it's cold, that there is no sun, that it's foggy. Now that the sun is burning hot, they have a new refrain: that they're dying from the heat, and they lie around in the parks and squares, all spread out like corpses.

Liza would look at the face of each person who placed a card in her box, look at the name of the requester and the books requested, and try to guess what kind of person he or she was. Liza was tall and had long brown hair and an attractive smile. On hot days, she wore a short dress, a loose, fiery red T-shirt with a picture of a green clown in the middle of it, and an uplift brassiere. She often went barefoot and wore a lot of jewellery: two chains around her neck (a loose one and a stiff one), three bracelets on her forearm, and an ankle chain that decorated her bare left foot. She was used to men following her with their eyes. Let them – who cared about them: she had plenty of boys there in the student residence. Why spend three years with so many boys who were her age and were students like her if not to have fun with them?

That Saturday morning, the library was packed and tense – everyone was in a hurry. The library was open only half a day on Saturday and then it was closed till Monday. One had to seize the opportunity. Liza made no concessions about her playing-while-working, and continued to ponder about everyone who came to her, but briefly – as soon as she took a card from one reader the next one was already in line. In her mind, Liza divided the readers into categories: doctoral candidates, professors, writers, researchers for television stations, plain idlers, and more than a few lonely people who came looking for pleasure and perhaps to find nice people in the bright, round reading room instead of sitting at home in the great lonely city.

Every day that summer, a person came in whom she had not succeeded in classifying: he was middle-aged, short, and fat – a Jew with a big bald pate and glasses with thick lenses. He was always dressed in a suit with a tie and a waistcoat, even on a hot day like this. The pretence of being all dressed up was not successful. It was no use – he looked ragged and sloppy, and his clothes were not new. They should have been sent to clothing Heaven long ago. Middle-aged men would often try to hold a conversation with a pretty girl who took their book request slips, but not this man. He didn't even look at her – he just hurried back to his little table, always the same one, as if the world would come to an end if he lost a minute from work. It was clear from the slips all summer that this man was researching something to do with psychology. He would order many editions of the same works by Freud and Jung, and a number of rare books about hypnosis from the nineteenth century, almost all of them in German. She learned from the request slips that his name was R. Meyerowitz. At that point, Liza developed the kind of attraction to him that occurs between good looking young girls and not-so-good-looking, not-so-young, 'interesting' men, especially those who show not the least bit of interest in them – perhaps also the attraction that draws young Gentile female students in London to learned, middle-aged, continental-born Jews.

Liza would try to start a conversation with Meyerowitz:

"How are you today, Mister Meyerowitz?"

"I see that you know my name already. Thank you, I feel all right. Are the book slips properly made out?"

"Of course – I'm going to send them right in, and the books will be right back. Are you working on a book?"

"I'm working on what I'm working on – there's no lack of what to work on." He blew her off, and quickly fled. He was not a man who had time to carry on idle conversation with the girls who worked in the library.

Every day Liza tried various tricks to involve the man in a conversation, but it was a waste of effort.

"Surely you're a famous psychologist?"

"I am Meyerowitz. Are the slips properly made out?"
"Yes."

B.

That Saturday, Liza decided to have it out with Meyerowitz. When the bells rang – a sign that the library was about to close – Liza went to look up R. Meyerowitz in the London telephone book, hoping that there would not be more than one person with that name. There was indeed only one. The address was 111 Commercial Road, in Whitechapel. Indeed! She knew that Whitechapel was the famous poor district in East London where generations of immigrants had settled, and where the inhabitants speak that beautiful Cockney English that slips now and again into spontaneous rhyme. Liza had never been in Whitechapel, but she knew about the district from her London parents, who had lived there before moving to Wales before she was born. Now she had moved to London to study, and consequently she had no friends in the city. The day was young, nothing else on the program – let's go!

The plan was a simple one. She would wander past his house. If she should happen to run into him, she would say: "What a coincidence! You give me your request slips in the British Museum every day." In the worst case, she would just get a look at Whitechapel.

She went on foot to Euston Square underground station and took the Underground. She rode to Baker Street, and there, on Platform 5, she took the Whitechapel train. In about 20 minutes she was in Whitechapel. When she went out into the street, it didn't seem at all like London, like

England. It was an exotic new world. The street named Whitechapel was a gigantic one; the sidewalk, an unbelievably wide one, was full of stores, wagons and little shops – sort of a market in one of the ancient colonies. All sorts of poor people were wandering around. Old homeless people were pushing little wagons with all their possessions. Crowds of Bangladeshi women were going around in their long, colourful dresses. Beggars were standing around with the lower part of broken whisky bottles, begging for coins. In the street, they were speaking a lot louder and a lot faster than in central London, and indeed with the jolly Cockney accent.

She was thirsty, and went into the nearest tavern, a pub called The Red Lion, with a large hanging sign on which was painted a picture of a big red lion and asked for a Pepsi-Cola. After a moment, she was approached by an old, bearded Whitechapel resident with torn clothes and a head of long, wild hair. She grew frightened. He said to her in Whitechapel-style English:

"Don't be afraid, I won't do you any harm. You have two brothers and a sister, but not in London. You yourself are Welsh. You've come to Whitechapel because of love, is that not so?"

"God in Heaven! How did you know that I have two brothers and a sister? That they are not in London? About love, the answer is no, not exactly, but . . ."

"My name is Sean. Hereabouts they call me Sean the Leprechaun. If you bring me a glass of bitter, I will tell you your future. I am a professional – I don't take money for nothing."

Why not?

"I'll be right there." And she brought him a bitter from the bar. He was already sitting sedately at the table, like a well-known doctor who sits and waits for his patients to sit down.

"Well – what will happen?"

"You will have three children, two daughters and a son. The eldest will be born ten years from today."

"That's very interesting, but there's no way I can know whether you are right. The fact you told me correctly how many brothers and sisters I have was a trick! That I am Welsh you could surely tell from my accent. But you said something about my coming to Whitechapel and love – perhaps you can say something about that?"

"I don't see the matter very clearly. I see only that you have come here because of someone. It is not entirely sensible that you are coming to him – it's one of those obsessions that force people to follow a path that they themselves are not at all sure they want to follow because they don't know where it will lead. By the way, I want you to know that all kind of ancient forces live in Whitechapel that have disappeared completely from elsewhere on these British Isles."

"Can you tell me something more specific?"

"No. I can tell you only what I know. If you wish, I can give you Lamar's address not far from here. Lamar is a much greater fortune-teller than I am; spirits of the dead turn up at his table. I am nothing more than a pub-prophet. He is a Gypsy. With him, however, you won't get away with just a glass of beer – with him it will cost you. He has a crystal ball, two black cats, a snake from Malaysia, a winged mouse, and incense."

"No, I have no money – I'll stick with you, Sean."

"In that case, I'll tell you just one more thing. In a little box without a lock there are often things that are worth no less than those contained in a box with a lock."

"I don't understand."

"Neither do I. I'm just telling you what I see. I, myself, understand such things very poorly. I have to go now."

Liza shivered – the kind of shiver that means that one has just experienced something important. When Sean left, she felt a desire for whisky. Among the student revelers during the school year, she didn't drink very much. In the summer, during the hot days, she actually didn't touch alcohol, but precisely now she had an urge to drink a glassful. Right there, in the Red Lion, she ordered four more glasses, one after another, all whisky neat, with a side order of a packet of stale, over-salted nuts.

They rang the bell in the pub indicating that they were about to close for the mandatory afternoon shutdown period. She felt kind of foggy. It seemed to her that they were ringing the library bell again, that a big red lion was standing in the middle of the library. When she went out into the street, her head cleared a little, and she had a new desire: coffee. But first, the thought was rolling around in her head that she had come looking for some sort of Meyerowitz somewhere on Commercial Road.

C.

Liza asked a chubby woman who was selling radios on the street how to get to Commercial Road and then set out. A few minutes later, she arrived at Number 111, an old ruin of a building on the corner of Parfett Street. She went into the hallway. On the wall, next to the mailboxes, there was a framed list of the residents, with a filthy glass cover. Among the Asiatic, Muslim and English names there was a Jewish name, R. Meyerowitz. She waited out in the street for a half an hour in case by some miracle he would just then go in or come out.

Nothing.

Now she was back on the main street, Whitechapel. She went into the ABC cafeteria that was right next to the entrance to the underground station, bought a cup of coffee, and opened a book that she had brought with her. After she had been sitting in the cafeteria for nearly an hour, who should come in but Meyerowitz. He was the only man in the cafeteria who was wearing a suit. She noted that he went over to an empty table with a cheese sandwich and a cup of coffee. He opened a newspaper and immersed himself in it while he was eating, as if he were wearing a sign: Don't bother me!

She, however, was hopeful. At least there was no wife there – he was alone. She didn't dare to go over to him, or even to move to a closer table. The man ate a bit at a time and read intensely, often adjusting his glasses, with their thick lenses. Liza held the empty cup of coffee in her hand and just looked.

Finally, the short, middle-aged Jew went out of the cafeteria. Liza followed him at a distance. He stopped at the corner, at a red light, and there she accosted him.

"Mister Meyerowitz! Surely you recognize me – I take your request slips every day in the British Museum."

"Yes, yes – I recognize you. Do you live here in this neighbourhood?"

"Uh, no, but I like this neighbourhood very much – I come here often," she babbled, just to say something.

"Where are you going now?"

"Uh, it's like this. I want to go to the river, the Thames. Can I get there through Commercial Road?"

"You can. I live on Commercial Road and I am going home. Perhaps you'd like to have a cup of coffee at my place?"

"Yes, thank you. It would be an honour for me."

"It's not an honour – it's coffee."

She walked with him for a few minutes. Poor children were playing with a rope that was tied to an upper-storey window on both sides of the little street. Each child flew across the street holding onto the rope. Meyerowitz said to his young companion:

"These children will grow up to be people who are capable of anything in the world. The well dressed, polite, neatly barbered children in Hampstead and the other wealthy neighbourhoods will grow up to be losers who speak with a beautiful accent and that's all; each of them a no-good, flabby nothing."

"Yes, you're right. But nevertheless, these kids could fall down and get killed."

They went into the building. Meyerowitz lived on the third storey. The staircase was narrow, dirty, and smelled of urine. Children were playing on the steps, speaking Bengali. Finally, when they were standing at his door, he took out a bunch of old-fashioned keys and opened it.

Inside Meyerowitz's apartment, things were even more of a ruin than in the corridors. No repairs had been done in many years. Where pieces of plaster had fallen off the wall, there were islands of light blue, yellow, and purple flowers, dirty white, and more than anything else – many shades of green. There were books everywhere, not on real shelves but on various boards that were supported on an assortment of cement blocks. The books were arranged carefully. Meyerowitz asked Liza to sit down on the only chair in the room, an old wooden chair with eight spokes in the back, of which two were missing. He went into the kitchen to make coffee. A little dog was sleeping on a piece of wallpaper that was so dusty that it was hard to decipher what colour it was. The dog looked very old, perhaps 120 in dog years.

"Surely, you're a student at London University."

"Yes. I've finished one year, majoring in English Literature. I work in the British Museum in the summers. I hope to be able to work there after the summer on the three evenings when the library is open late. I like the way your apartment is full of books."

"I'm unemployed, but my life is study. Before the war, I was a student of psychology at the university in Vilna. Have you ever heard of Vilna?"

"It rings a bell. Where is it exactly?"

"It's the crown city of Lithuania, historically speaking, but was part of Poland between the two World Wars, when I was growing up. I am a Jew. During the war, I ended up in the concentration camp Buchenwald, with my two young sons; my wife had already been shot in the forest of Ponar, not far from Vilna. A small number of Jews who were young and strong enough to work were taken to the camps in Germany rather than being shot in the forest of Ponar, so in this crazy world I was saved by being sent to a death camp, where death didn't come as quickly as it did at the local shooting sites. In the camp, the Nazis put up wire fences, different for children of every age. Since I am short, my sons were short; their heads didn't reach the top of the wire fences, so they were promptly sent to the gas chamber. England is a fantastic country – they give me this apartment and I can study and write all day long. My life's work is a book about hypnosis in the nineteenth century and its influence on Freud. Freud later dismissed hypnosis with a wave of his hand when he formulated psychoanalysis, but without hypnosis there would have been no Freud and certainly no psychoanalysis. The name of the book will be: 'No Hypnosis – No Freud'."

"That's very interesting," said Liza, but as she spoke, she realized that she was still a bit tipsy and barely understood what the man was talking about. She wasn't ashamed to ask whether he had whisky in the apartment. Though he had just brought her coffee and was standing next to her – he hadn't brought in another chair for himself – he went back into the kitchen and in an instant came back with a bottle of cognac and two big wine glasses, rather than shot-glasses. From the amount of dust on the bottle, it was clear that it had been yearning for a guest to lift the mood in the lonely apartment for quite a few years. Liza suddenly exclaimed: "I've been, well, very interested in you all summer, if I may ask you to forgive me for being so forward."

"What are you talking about? I'm old and ugly, and you are young and pretty. There aren't enough young men for you at the university?"

"There are enough of them."

"I'm very sorry – you're a very fine person and an extraordinarily pretty girl, but I have remained faithful to my murdered wife all my life. After her death, I swore an oath that I wouldn't look at another woman, in the sense of 'as a woman', till the day of my death."

"Yes, I understand. Can we perhaps be just friends?"

"By all means. I would be happy to have a young friend, or rather a lady friend. Listen – I have to leave soon, but when we meet in the library on Monday we'll arrange to have lunch in the West End, in central London. OK?"

"Good, thanks."

"I'll walk you out to the street."

D.

In the street the sun was still burning hot. Liza was filled with the whisky, with the prophet from the pub, and with the short Jew who didn't want to love her. A strange place, Whitechapel. A crazy man was standing on the corner. Despite the heat, he was wearing a coat, boots, and gloves. As Liza was passing by, he called out to her:

"My dear girl – lunacy! Only lunacy is sane! Down with clear-minded people – to Hell with them!"

She smiled and continued on her way. An old, rumpled man was trying to fix a hole in the wheel of a bicycle with two tin-can covers, and while doing that he was rumbling an English song under his breath: "I'm Henry the Eighth, I am." In the Whitechapel way, he said 'Enerry, not Henry.

A group of happy Jews were following a handsome Jew with a magnetic smile and a sensual voice. He had the face of royalty, but was wearing the clothes of poverty – old, poor clothes.

They were speaking a foreign language, probably Yiddish. Each tried to attract his attention – calling out to him in a single voice: "Shtentsl!" Apparently, his name was Shtentsl. As he passed by, Liza stared at him enchanted. She walked down a small side-street, back towards the subway station. Two young Whitechapelers, English worker types, asked her whether she wanted to come inside their place. It was very jolly inside, they assured her. Liza thought about it for a moment, lifted her head obliquely, and looked at a distant high window where a child was playing on the platform of a fire-escape right next to the window.

"Why not?" These were not bad fellows, she thought.

They led her through the door of an old building. From the outside, it looked somewhat of a ruin; the inside was freshly painted in all kinds of colours, as if random – here there was a square of yellow on a green wall, there a shapeless collage of red on a blue wall. There was every colour except black and white. The parlour was full of young men and young women; all of them were drinking and smoking, carousing at the top of their voices. The two victorious boys went in with their captured little fish, Liza. She was pretty, and a student in the bargain. Liza realized immediately that this was a really jolly group, not the spoiled students that considered themselves bigshot scholars there in the university.

"What are you studying there in the *universitee*?"

"Uh – English literature," she murmured, knowing full well that that would only be a big joke to the gang in Whitechapel.

"And I clean houses," a girl with half-blond, half-green hair, a ring in her nose, and an earring in her right ear called out.

"I steal cars," proudly declared a short, skinny boy wearing a black leather jacket. "Anyone who is so stingy that he doesn't have an alarm in his car has no right to have a car. I sell them immediately and they ship them away to Poland before the police here realize that a car is missing. Of course, here and there we have to turn a car over to the local police. After all, something is owed to them too."

"Eddie is famous. I'm only a waitress in a café near here."

"Shush – I have a plan," said Simon, the tallest, handsomest boy in the crowd. He had black hair that looked as if he had dunked it in no more and no less than a whole bottle of dye. "Let our new friend Liza abandon her foolishness with English literature – is that what she called it or not? – and become my girlfriend. I've needed a girlfriend since my previous one – that's her, Polly, standing over there – threw me out like a used-up shmeckeldecker!* And for whom did she throw me out? For what big bargain? For ugly Bob! There he stands, he does – Bob! Dirty dogs, both of them! Oh well – that's yesterday's story. I'm not a person who suffers from those things. I think it's time I should have a girlfriend from the *universitee*. Fellows! I have an important announcement. True, we've all had a lot to drink, but I'm not a man who speaks just like that." And he turned to Liza, went down on one knee, and said to her with no nonsense:

---

* Shmekldeker, Yiddish slang for a condom.

"Liza! I love you! Leave all that nonsense there in the *universitee* and come be my lady. I have a beautiful flat I do, around here, not far from the river. My friends will be your friends; all that's mine will be yours. What do you say?"

"Uh, hee-hee. I've had a whole lot to drink today, and I don't know what I'm saying, but – OK! Done! Here there seems to be some real joy, not like with our pompous pricks there in the *universitee*," she said, trying to learn the locally standard rendition of this word of scorn. "And as for literature – it's idiotic, after all, to read what they tell you to."

And immediately the London student entered into a contest with the Whitechapel youth to see who was bolder and more daring, who was more of a 'real person'.

"I'm staying in Whitechapel!" Liza cried out.

"Bravo!" the whole gang cried out with one great voice, and they started dousing her with a bottle of wine.

That night they caroused till very late. After that they drove, ten of them, in three cars, to Liza's room at the university, picked up her belongings, and took them to Simon's flat in Whitechapel, and there she stayed. She worked with Simon in his shop, where he sold used furniture (some of it made into 'antiques' for the benefit of sloanies who came to these parts looking for antiques in East London). She learned from Simon how to clean everything with old towels and rub it with linseed oil, and then bee's-wax till it shone. She turned junk into antiques. Things went better and better for them. She told her parents in Wales that they didn't have to send any more money. Two years went by, and Simon printed a diploma from somewhere. Liza sent it to her parents so they would not be disappointed, and that was that. English literature would get along without her.

E.

As soon as Liza left Meyerowitz's flat that Saturday, he was struck by a pang of regret. Yes love, no love – who rejects a beautiful young girl who comes and declares her interest in a fat, old Jew like him? And what sense did it make to tell her a fairy tale about having to go someplace? What harm would it have done if she had sat for another half-hour? His sainted wife herself would have said that. But he reminded himself that he would see Liza in the Library on Monday. Not so terrible. Then he would invite her for a nice lunch somewhere.

Monday morning, Meyerowitz got out of bed with unusual vigour. For the first time, he washed his remaining hair twice, exactly as directed on the shampoo bottle. For the first time since he had come to London, he didn't buy a newspaper at the entrance to the Underground station in Whitechapel. He entered the great, round reading hall as usual, ran to the catalogue cards in the centre, and quickly wrote order cards for several books. He didn't look up. After that, he went confidently to the little window where one lays the cards. But someone else was already sitting there.

The Ring

A.

At work they called Basil Cartwright 'The Robot'. He was middle-aged and of medium height and build. He had an expressionless face, hands that made no gestures, and eyes that held no secrets. His gait was like that of a marionette and his voice was like that of someone who reads the news over the radio. His stinginess with words, however, was that of the eternal bureaucrat who was born to work in an office. He wore grey suits and old-fashioned black shoes with many perforations for ventilation. He wore glasses that were neither round nor square but something in between. Like his face – indescribable.

Basil Cartwright was responsible for keeping the inventory. He recorded on his computer everything that came into or went out of the large Rymans stationery store on Tottenham Court Road, a broad, not-very-pretty avenue in central London. Those who worked there called it 'Totters,' and they called Basil Cartwright 'The Robot of Totters.'

In earlier years, he had written everything down in a large ledger with many columns. Now he had finally found a friend, as it were – a face-like screen, a keyboard heart, and a mouse-like hand to hold. One robot felt a closeness with another.

From the top boss to the man who washed the floors, the workers in the store were a lazy bunch, but they devoted a lot of energy to finding tricks for working as little and flirting as much as possible. They were not even ashamed of it – they were dealing with paper, envelopes, pens, cards, and address-books, not matters of life and death, and customers could wait. The store belonged to a big company somewhere far away, and they didn't care either, as long as the annual profit was satisfactory. Writing implements and paper-goods – as long as they had in their stocks more, better, and cheaper things than other stores, everything 'sold itself,' so they didn't even look for anyone who was very ambitious. They took people who were young and good-looking, wore clean clothing, and gave the impression that they were satisfied with life. Business psychologists have demonstrated by statistical studies that those are the kind that people buy from, not compulsive workers, geniuses, and deep thinkers, all of whom are very neurotic. Only the inventory-keeper and the bookkeeper had to be highly capable workers.

The 'Robot of Tottenham' never went out partying. He never touched alcohol. No one ever saw him laugh. He was one of those born bachelors whose work is their whole life, who have no desire to chatter with people about trivial matters.

Every year, in August, Basil Cartwright went on vacation for two weeks. Where he went, or whether he left London at all, no one knew. That year, when he came back to the store from his vacation, he was wearing a round little ring on his finger. Everyone stared at it. For months they spoke of only one thing among themselves – had the robot gotten married? The expressionless face, the hands without gestures, the eyes without secrets were the same as always, not those of a middle-aged bachelor who had just gotten married. And Basil Cartwright was one of those Englishmen who radiate the message that one doesn't dare talk to them about matters personal.

When the December season of fun and games came, the workers in the stationery store decided they had to get to the bottom of the matter. Their leader was Annie, a pretty youngish woman with a broad smile, brown hair, and charming freckles. She kept everyone entertained all day with her clever remarks. She played flirtatious games with all the men there, except Basil Cartwright – 'dated' them, as they called it there. She'd break it off with one of them and turn to another. But no one had any hard feelings – there was no lack of people to 'date'.

"I'll find out," Annie told the gang, with the tone of a princess of the paper-world in the centre of London. Boldly, she went up to Basil Cartwright.

"Basil! Such a beautiful ring! I hadn't noticed it before. Excuse me – is it new? Did you . . ."

"Thank you, Annie," he interrupted with his radio-announcer's voice, glancing meanwhile at the ring out of the corner of his eye. The glance both confirmed that the ring was there and also informed her that he would have nothing more to say on that topic. He continued, as if in the same sentence: "Am I not correct that someone stole two nibs for a #44 pen from your counter this week? Please confirm that – I have to complete this darned inventory today."

Now that Annie had dared to ask and had been repulsed, everyone's curiosity about the ring turned into an obsession. And if he had gotten married, who could have wanted to marry such a person? Was she young or old, pretty or ugly, an Englishwoman or a foreigner?

Obsessions lead to actions. The same Annie had a brother who was a policeman. Despite the fact that she only worked in a stationery store and was no government minister, she still looked down on her brother – his name was James. Though they had been brought up in the same house, Annie spoke with an elegant upper-class English accent, and he spoke with a rather common one.

She presented her brother with the story about the 'robot' and his ring as a good-humoured challenge. James was disappointed.

"Some story! I'll get you an answer by tomorrow. Next time don't insult me in front of the boys, you hear? Bring us a real challenge, not some childish nonsense. Did some man in the stationery store get married? Don't you have anything more interesting to investigate there?"

B.

James immediately checked the list of all marriages in his computer. Basil Cartwright hadn't gotten married. Basil Cartwright hadn't brought in a bride from a foreign country.

That evening, one of James' colleagues showed up on the

street where Basil Cartwright's apartment was located and began questioning the neighbours discreetly. They hadn't ever seen Basil Cartwright go into or out of his apartment with anyone, either man or woman.

That night, James telephoned his sister and told her that there was no longer any mystery. Basil Cartwright had never gotten married, he lived alone in the same apartment as always, and no one went into his house, either man or woman.

"So why is he suddenly wearing a ring?"

"How should I know? Probably because he likes it! There are some strange people in your store. A man gets an urge to buy a ring, and you all cook up a story that he must have gotten married. Next time bring me a mystery and not some nonsense! You hear?"

"But you don't see men wearing rings just like that!"

"So, you don't see them! Do I know? It's the wildest thing I've ever heard of in my life! You've all been working with him there all these years and you're ashamed to ask him whether it's a gift. You don't have to mention marriage – just ask him!"

"It's not possible. There's no opportunity to do so. He doesn't answer."

"I have to go. Look after yourself, little sister!"

But the truth was that by now James couldn't get his sister's question out of his mind all night: a man lives alone, he's a perfect bureaucrat, and suddenly he's wearing a ring. It didn't make sense. To smooth over his embarrassment about sniffing around some more into the private life of an honest person, he thought up an excuse: it was a good exercise – it might happen that they would have to find out such information in relation to a real crime, a stolen ring; who could tell?

The next day, in the morning, James went himself to Basil Cartwright's flat. He went in uniform. He knocked on the door. It was an hour before Basil Cartwright usually went to work, but he was already shaven and dressed in *his* uniform, the grey suit with the black, perforated shoes. But there was no ring on his finger!

The young policeman was used to telling lies in the same automatic way that Basil Cartwright was used to telling the truth.

"Excuse me Mr. Cartwright? I'm sorry to bother you about a trivial matter. A woman here in the neighbourhood, probably a crazy person, keeps telephoning the police. She says you found a gold ring that she lost. I'm sure that's simply nonsense, but I had to come and ask you. Just tell me where and when you got your ring and whether it was a gift from someone, and we'll be rid of this nuisance of a lady who won't leave us alone."

"That's fine, officer," said Basil Cartwright, smiling broadly. "First of all, it's not gold – it's a cheap thing. If there's a woman nearby who wants it, I'll give it to her right now. Secondly, I didn't find it – I bought it last summer when I went on vacation. You'll laugh – I bought it as a joke, so my co-workers in the store would have something to chatter about. They are unbelievably boring people. They all walk around like robots, talk like robots, so I played a little joke with the ring, for a bit of amusement at work. You see that I don't wear it at home. If you'd like to take a look at it, I can show it to you right now. Wait a minute . . ."

"No, no! It's not necessary. Thank you, Sir, and excuse me for bothering you so early. Good-bye."

"Good-bye, Officer."

The Bird in the Letterbox

A.

Greville Bond never closed his eyes that night. Nevertheless, he wasn't at all tired when he got out of bed in the morning, he just had a slight headache, which he had almost deliberately developed in order to soothe a horrible grief somewhat with a lesser, temporary affliction.

It was his last day of work in the big Anderson and Williamson spectacle-store in central London. Just before five-thirty in the evening, they closed the two opposing glass doors and began bringing in bottles of wine and a large cake, on which 65 whitish-grey candles were mourning. They gave Greville Bond a gold watch with a chain, and on the watch was engraved his name and the years of faithful work for Anderson and Williamson.

His co-worker, Peggy Granville, a spinster about 50 years old, pudgy with light-brown hair streaked with long white strands, wore the frozen half-smile of a sad old maid. She gazed with pain at the widower, who hadn't responded at all to her flirtatious gestures. And now he was leaving. Although she was there together with everyone, it seemed as if she were sitting alone, like a widow, in a corner of the room. She was wearing her favourite dress, a white one with bluish checks.

And there, hanging around him, was their young co-worker, Nia Evans, a little firebrand, Welsh with a head of too-closely-cropped blond hair. At the age of twenty-five she was already grieving bitterly about a former lover, like an old, discarded girl-friend. Greville Bond's distant, dispassionate look attracted her, and her disappointed eyes tried to tell the widower: "You could at least be friendly, you know."

The big boss, Mister Williamson, a skinny little pipsqueak with gigantic black spectacles – that was all one remembered about his face – made a speech praising Greville Bond. But the speech failed to mention the one thing on everyone's mind, that Greville was the only one who personally remembered the story, rather than just hearing about it from customers, about Mister Willamson and his historic partner whose surname joined his in the business's moniker. He was also the one and only person who could still remember the co-founder, his partner Anderson, whom Williamson had used and then discarded, utilizing all the sly manoeuvres of the polite English courts.

"Greville Bond is more than a dear colleague and friend to all of us. He is the embodiment of professionalism, loyalty to the firm, and striving for excellence. The fact that our firm has built itself up from a tiny business to this large, famous enterprise is largely due to him. I won't make a long speech – we'd all rather talk to Greville! To Greville! To wish him a long, happy future. I'll just mention the first thing I learned from him when he came to work here twenty-six years ago: he immediately pointed out to me that one mustn't pressure a customer; let him walk around by himself, pick up whatever spectacle-frames appeal to him, and only when he, the customer himself, stops for a longer time at a frame that really suits him should one go up to him and tell him how handsome he looks, or how pretty she looks, if it be a lady. Thanks to Greville Bond's wisdom, we expanded. We look forward to his friendship and advice in future years. We wish him health and success in everything he does."

"Greville!" He raised his glass slightly with a relaxed, self-assured motion. Just slightly, the lack of energy indicating, as it were, that the boss had no intention whatever of pretending that he believed his own prattling.

"GRE-ville!" they shouted with a thunderous combined voice. From the almost outlandish enthusiasm, a bystander would have thought that they were very happy to be rid of the old-timer. In reality, the younger folk simply took advantage of the toasts to do some mild flirting. The older senior managerial personnel talked about business matters and showed off with such-and-such figures.

In the course of an hour and a half of guzzling and chattering, Greville Bond, in the eyes of his colleagues, gradually became transformed from a distinguished colleague into a living corpse who was no longer a person and would putter around uselessly in his house till one day his body would cease to function. By the time they got to the farewell toast, the young man they had employed in his place was already hovering about like a locust.

Greville Bond was used to going home at five-thirty, when the underground cars were crowded with squeezed-together people. Now it was getting on to nine o'clock and the car was almost empty, so it frivolously and airily bounded along the rails, like a goat skipping over the mountains. Seated in the car was another pair of 'unneeded' people who were in no hurry to go anywhere, whose enthusiasm for what life may hold was similarly extinguished.

Sitting in the car, he felt bad momentarily about his wife, who had changed from a person into a corpse about five years earlier. And his thoughts strayed involuntarily to his co-worker Peggy Granville, who had desired him and whom he had repulsed with pure coldness, as if she were guilty of his wife's sudden demise. And even more involuntarily, there came to him in the car the face of young Nia Evans, whose innocent invitations to a most innocent cup of tea he had been unable to accept under any circumstances.

No more Peggy, no more Nia, no more work, no more spectacles-salesman.

Now he would no longer refuse anyone's invitation.

The stocky, medium-height Greville Bond began to mourn his remaining years. With the four long fingers of his right hand he stroked his thick grey hair from front to back, wondering meanwhile how a man of his age could suddenly put on a brand-new face. The thought made him even more melancholy. He was now a 'used-to-be', facing an endless series of empty days – every day a cup of sorrow.

And stiff Greville Bond began to sob, not at all like Greville Bond.

Out of the car, up the stairs, down the stairs. Peggy, Nia, empty days – his thoughts (of their own volition – Greville no longer had any power over them) returned continually to his wife, who had died suddenly on him. In life she hadn't ever gone to see him at work – that was his thing, you know! If only she were waiting for him at home today with a bottle of French wine! Afterwards they would go on vacation, somewhere sunny where no London damp could reach. And now he was going home to an empty house, to loneliness and sorrow. He could look forward to only two things on the medium and distant horizon: illness and death.

Shuffling at a leisurely pace, he walked home. For a brief moment he started to think – he himself and not some angel and not some stray thought – about something that could lift his spirits. What would happen if he went into a theatrical supply house, rented a wig and a really wild disguise, and went into Anderson and Williamson to ask, with a disguised voice, for spectacle frames. Huh? Huh?

Right near his house, he took a coin out of his pocket to buy the evening paper, but the man who sold them every evening at six o'clock was not there.

Greville Bond went up the steps to his house with the gait of one who had just gotten old.

He turned the first, big, old-fashioned key and opened the first lock. Turned the second, small modern little key – turned it to the right and at the same time turned the doorknob. Went into the dark hall. Turned on the light switch and walked down the hall of his house.

Suddenly, he saw lying on the floor a multicoloured bird, as beautiful as an unexpected rainbow.

The bird was perfectly formed, without a blemish, without an injury. He bent down and examined it more closely. He poked it with the tip of his shoe, to see whether the multicoloured bird would wake up from its bird-sleep and fly away, as birds do.

The bird was as dead as a doornail. For an instant he saw before him his suddenly deceased wife.

In her, too, there had been no injury to be seen. The bird, in its rigidity, radiated a certain beauty that was unworldly in its perfect splendour.

Greville Bond let out a gasp. His head snapped back. His eyes looked at the old ceiling. Cold shivers ran up his spine, one after another. He went out into the backyard to get a shovel, came back into the hall, picked up the bird, and shovelled it into a black sack. He opened the two locks, carried the sack outside to the front of the house, and threw it with disgust into the tin garbage-can. The sack now contained an ugly corpse, not some perfect creature in its eternal rest.

He went back inside, locked the front door with both locks, poured himself a glass of whisky and poured it down his throat at one gulp. His whole body was bathed in sweat. He took off his jacket and sat down on the couch. His head was still clear, too clear, and in his imagination he saw the dead bird on the floor. He hadn't gotten drunk for many years, but now he just wanted to fall into a deep sleep. He poured himself another glass and then another, till he fell into a drunken slumber on the couch. He didn't have to worry about getting up the next day.

The next morning, Greville Bond got out of bed full of hope and energy, not at all like a newly retired person who had found a dead bird in his house and had put himself to sleep with a bottle of whisky. He bathed, shaved, and got dressed up in a suit, as he did every other day of the year. Instead of selling spectacle-frames, he had a new assignment: figure the thing out – how did a dead bird come to be on his floor? Wearing his suit, he felt ready for anything. He rejoiced silently that life had given him a new assignment, immediately, on the first day of his retirement. There was, after all, a God in Heaven!

The suit his armour, Greville Bond climbed up a ladder to the attic to check whether a roof-tile had fallen out. The trapdoor leading from the hall into the attic had in fact been open for several weeks. No light from outside was visible in the attic. No bird could have come in there.

It was a chilly, early spring day, and all the windows were still closed from the day before. He was again assailed by fear and chills.

He considered all the possibilities and was left with only one: someone had thrown in a dead bird through the letter box.

He had found the bird rather far from the letter box, but in a straight line from it, exactly in the middle of the hall. A quick hand thrust through the wide letter box, holding the dead bird, had thrown the corpse as far into the house as it could. The straight line couldn't have been an accident. Some enemy of his had played an ugly trick on him, to warn him, perhaps even to threaten him with murder. Such tricks weren't carried out by cripples – someone who was good at throwing things had thrown it far into the hall. Ugh!

Greville Bond remembered the gangster movies: they would send a dead rat to someone they were going to murder. It's only a short step from a dead rat to a bird. Poking a hand through someone's letter box and throwing such an ugly thing into his house was more audacious, more threatening than sending filth through the mail. That's how Greville Bond looked at it.

He went to the nearby police station and told them what had happened. They asked him whether he had any enemies, and whether he hadn't gotten into a quarrel, small or large, with a lover, another boy-friend of a lover, or even some customer in the big spectacle-store from which he had just retired. He couldn't think of anything. Till five years ago, he had been a faithful husband. After that – alone. He certainly didn't have any enemies at work. On the contrary, when a customer was dissatisfied with his glasses, he, Greville Bond, had instituted a policy of exchanging them gratis for others that he liked. He had even taught the big boss that with unusually nice treatment one gains a permanent customer, and all others whom that customer deigns to recommend to the establishment, and in the end earns a lot more than by disappointing people.

He told the police that the previous day had been his last on the job in the big Anderson and Williamson spectacle-store in the centre of the city. The two policemen who listened to all of this strongly doubted that Greville Bond was in his right mind. They looked at one another with a bit of a wink, as if to say that here was a lonely person who wanted attention. One of the policemen interrupted him and asked whether the dead bird was still there. Greville answered that he had carried it out in a black sack and put it into the tin garbage-can in the street, which had probably already been emptied that morning.

The second policeman, who had been writing everything down in the police ledger, took a look at the long line of people who were waiting to report robberies, lost items, various crimes, and all sorts of civic ills and problems. He abruptly terminated the interview and told Greville Bond that if nothing further happened he should forget about the unpleasant incident. London was a big city, and there were more than a few harmless nuts wandering around. If something did happen, he should come back to them. They, for their part, would again check out the matter on their computers and find out whether there was some crazy person in the neighbourhood who was throwing dead birds through letter boxes. Was there any lack of crazy things in London?

He left the police station. He bought a notebook in a stationery store. He went with the notebook to a nearby café. It was his first time in a café on a weekday morning. He began to write down a list of possible enemies in the notebook. About forty years earlier, even before he had gotten to know his wife, he had left a girlfriend after promising to marry her. He had an older brother to whom he hadn't spoken in many years, because of a quarrel about their father's small legacy, but his brother had been in New Zealand for decades – if he had stayed in London, they would have long since gotten back on good terms.

He wrote down everything, thinking meanwhile that every person had quarrels and enemies in his time – one just had to think about it. Nevertheless, the more he thought about it the clearer it became that it would never have occurred to any of them to throw a dead bird through the letter box at this particular juncture in time. It was a wild thing to do. He was plagued by the conclusion that it couldn't possibly be an accident that such an ugly thing had been done to him precisely on the day of his retirement. Ugh!

He walked around the street, afraid to go back home lest someone again throw a dead animal through his letter box, but when he fearfully unlocked the two locks that evening, there were on the floor only two advertising circulars that had been thrown into every house on the block.

When he had left his job for the last time, he had been afraid that the days would start creeping like years. But they were running away more quickly. A year passed, and two years, and three years. Nothing. His days as well as his nights became foggy – transformed into a drawn-out twilight, a personal abyss. It was a life in which nothing happened. The daily activities – shopping, cooking, walking around, cleaning up – were unconscious and automatic.

If not for the fact that he spent every day thinking about the question of who had thrown the dead bird through the letter box, he wouldn't have been thinking at all. He would have not been a person, just a body that carried on the daily activities that are necessary so that the gears of the machine keep turning. Every now and then he smiled and thought to himself that it was only thanks to the great question that he had anything at all to think about in his old age.

Greville Bond's rumination, however, was an example of the kind of obsessions that don't let a person rest. Five years passed, and now that he was seventy years old, he decided to see a doctor, who asked him about his life. He immediately entrusted the doctor with the information that on the day he retired someone had thrown a dead bird into his letter box.

The doctor referred him to a psychiatrist, and told him gently that he was referring him, not because there was any suspicion that the story of the dead bird was not true, but for a very practical reason; the psychiatrist would help him make sense of it all. After all, making sense of it all would be a good thing. Greville Bond went to the psychiatrist about two weeks later. The tall, young doctor with long blond hair and small round glasses listened to him, interrogated him, and finally suggested a treatment.

"You have been very unfortunate in that precisely on the day of your retirement five years ago, some crazy person did such a terrible thing to you. It's entirely normal that such a thing should torment you – it's only human and it's to be expected. I'm only sorry that you didn't come to me sooner. What can I tell you? The greatest strength of the human spirit is to draw good from evil, success from failure, ideas from stray thoughts. So, listen to me; you'll be much happier in your house if you buy a little pet, a kitten or a puppy, perhaps a beautiful bird. What do you say?"

Greville Bond thanked the psychiatrist half-heartedly and went home. He had always been extremely careful about the rigorous cleanliness of his house – he had no desire for a pet.

When he went out into the street – this was in central London, not very far from Anderson and Willamson – Greville Bond promptly forgot about the bird, about the five years, and about the psychiatrist's advice. During his trip home on the Underground, he suppressed any thoughts about what had happened on the night of his retirement.

B.

It occurred to him that he might visit his old store after five years, so he went there and went in.

Everyone rejoiced to see him. "Greville" here and "Greville" there". Where have you been? Why did you disappear? This was not just a formality – it was from the heart, like at the retirement party.

It was just before lunch time. "Greville – lunch!" everyone started to call out.

To make it interesting for him, they went to a new restaurant, which hadn't existed when he retired.

At lunch, over a glass of wine, young Nia burst out laughing, gave him to understand that his 'lover that never was', Penny Granville, had left the store several years ago, disappointed that even after his retirement and after her wonderfully conceived gift he had never contacted her. While Nia was still talking, she realized that she wouldn't have dared talk about such personal matters while he was working in the store.

Greville, in a loud and somewhat angry voice, hardly the old Greville's, exclaimed:

"Gift? What gift? The watch was everyone's gift after all!"

"Who's talking about the watch? I mean the bird! She bought a caged bird for you, imported from Sri Lanka, I think, and carried it to your house by taxi so she would get there before you did by the underground. She took the bird out of the cage and put it into your house through the letter box. She left the cage right next to the door, together with a note in which she wrote lots of lovely things and her telephone number. She waited for you to telephone her, but she waited in vain."

"There was no cage in front of the door! And certainly no note!"

"What are you saying? Maybe someone stole it. After all, London is not at all what it used to be. Do you still have the bird? How long does a bird live?"

"I found it dead, on the floor of the hallway. All these years I've been sure that someone threw a dead bird into my house, and on the day of my retirement!"

"No, no, no! It cannot be! Blimey! And Penny couldn't understand why you never got in touch with her, at least to say thank you, even if you didn't want to go out with her."

"I went to the police. I thought it was a threat, like with a dead rat in those gangster films."

Everyone broke out laughing, except Greville Bond – Greville broke out into a sweat. When they noticed that the story was anguishing him, they immediately changed the subject and started babbling about store business.

When it came time to say good-bye and Greville was about to return to his retirement abyss, he quietly asked Nia for Penny's telephone number.

That evening, after rehearsing dozens of times what he would say to her, he dialed the numbers on his old-fashioned rotary-dial phone. When Penny picked up the receiver, Greville immediately began to stammer and got his words all mixed up.

"Greville! Is my bird still alive?"

"But I found it dead! I thought some enemy of mine had thrown in an ugly dead creature, just like they send someone a dead rat in the movies."

"No, no! It cannot be! Blimey!"

"I went to the police."

When she heard the word 'police', Penny erupted in laughter.

"A fine man! I leave you a beautiful gift and instead of telephoning me and saying 'Thank You' you go to the police. The cage and the note weren't there?"

"Not there."

There was a long silence, till Greville Bond also erupted in laughter, laughter like that of ten years earlier. He hadn't allowed himself a good laugh for the five years after his wife's death and for another five years after the bird's death.

Penny plucked up her courage, as if to make up for the wasted years.

"Now we can be good friends."

"So, when shall we go out on a date?"

"Today."

"By all means!"

The Proofreader

A.

Till the age of 18, the life of Mere-Dov, the watchmaker's son, was a quiet one. In his hometown of Smargon, in the province of Vilna, he studied a year in *kheyder* and the rest of the time in the leftist secular Yiddish schools of the *Tse-Be-Ka* system (the Yiddish schools of the Central Education Committee.) Later he became an apprentice in a print-shop. When, in the late 1930's, in the year after Pilsudski's death, he saw some drunken Polish soldiers beating up a Jew in the street late one Saturday night, for no reason and with no conversation or quarrel, he left for Vilna with a former teacher and joined a group of revolutionaries who occupied the attic apartment of an abandoned country house in the Antokl district. He fell in love and promptly got married to a girl there – Sorke. In Vilna, he called himself Max Triebwasser. For him, the smell of Fascism was in the air, and it wasn't long before he went to London with his wife to the home of his eldest brother, Ben, who had resided there for some ten years.

The London brother, who had never married, ran a business of old stamps in Fulham Road. He awaited Max and his wife with great excitement at Liverpool Street station. He recognized his younger brother from photographs and began yelling "Merke! Merke!" at the top of his lungs. The brothers danced a little dance of joy in the station and kissed each other so effusively on the lips, as was the custom, that the surrounding Brits, who were not used to that, began staring discreetly out of the corners of their eyes as they walked past.

Ben took Max and Sorke to his rented flat, with three large rooms directly over the stamp store. In London, Sorke (formerly Sarah) became Cecilia. Later on, during the early days of the German blitzkrieg, when the prices of houses started sinking like a lead balloon, the brother bought the store and the flat for a pittance. Collectors who would die for a certain rare stamp were not going to be intimidated by the fear of bombs falling from the skies.

An old Jewish neighbour advised Max that since he had worked in a printing shop in the old country and didn't know a word of English, he should go down to the Yiddish printing shops in Whitechapel to look for work, and that he should start with Naroditsky's. Naroditsky had no work for him. Max knocked around in Whitechapel for an afternoon till a Jew in a café told him to go to the editorial offices of the daily Yiddish newspaper. The janitor immediately took him up to the editor, Morris Mayer, who gave him a wry smile and told the young man that his proofreader had just died and none of the other writers wanted to go back to that hated work. Max Triebwasser, with an almost boyish pride, told him that in Smargon he had more than once helped the old proofreader of sacred writings in the print shop, and that afterwards, in Vilna, he had become familiar with the styles and requirements of the modern Socialist papers. Morris Mayer took him on for a month's trial. No further printing errors needing correction were found in the newspaper, which had previously been something of a laughing-stock to visiting foreign Yiddish authors and intellectuals because of its multitudinous typos.

Max had no head for understanding the meaning of a line of print, but he knew how to spell in all styles. He had learned the secret of proofreading from working as a boy with sacred Hebrew and Aramaic commentaries on the Bible and Talmud, from the old Smargon proofreader of sacred writings, who taught him to read every line backward and every page from the end to the beginning, so he would look at words, not sentences. If it was Hebrew or Aramaic, he did not have to understand any of it – he just compared each word with the manuscript or older edition that was the source, also backward, running his eyes from full stop to full stop, comma to comma. After that, one would proceed to whole phrases, lines, and pieces that had been omitted or transposed. After a month, Morris Mayer raised his pitifully low wages and crowned him 'head proofreader', though there were no others, and finally, when the editor felt that even more recognition was necessary, he added the words 'head proofreader' on the list of writers in each day's paper.

The three Triebwassers in Fulham Road did not go hungry. Ben was the king of the stamp dealers in the neighbourhood.

Max was the head proofreader at the London daily Yiddish newspaper. Sorke quickly learned English in evening classes and went on to learn typing and stenography. She even got work as a secretary in the centre of the city, the West End. Foreign, and especially East European accents were so common after the war that nobody paid much attention to that. The years passed quickly.

B.

One morning, Max found his brother lying on the wooden floor of the store. He was unconscious and was breathing with the gasps of a dying man. A cream-yellow cardboard sheet with rows of transparent plastic pockets for stamps, which he was in the process of setting up in the glass show-window, lay on the floor. Dozens of stamps were scattered around. One beautiful blue stamp lay right on his lips as if it wanted to give the stamp dealer one last kiss. Synchronously with the too-rhythmical and too-heavy breathing brought on by the heart attack, the stamp went in and out of his mouth as if it had already become part of the dying man. After several days in the hospital in a coma, he died. People in the neighbourhood were astonished that such a healthy youngish man could die so suddenly.

Max and Cecilia, now just the two of them, continued to live in the flat, and they rented out the store to whoever came along – another stamp dealer for a few years and then a locksmith, who in the middle of the night often hammered and puttered around with old locks, butchers' knives, and pieces of the handsome cast-iron fences that the government had dismantled all over during the war years, for melting down and turning into ammunition.

One fine day, the Yiddish newspaper suddenly closed. The big building with the big clock that hinted at the name of the newspaper, 'The Times', was taken over by the Albion brewery. That day, Max came home pale and depressed. Dark thoughts ran through his mind. His entire family that had remained in Smargon had been killed. His brother had died young. He had lost his beloved job.

The following Sunday, Cecilia, utterly unable and unwilling to offer him comfort after his job loss, joined him for lunch in the West End, and without preliminaries told him that for several years she had been carrying on an affair with her boss, an elderly Englishman, a widower, and that she wanted to marry him. She needed a divorce. She would not take a penny from Max. She assured him in a relaxed tone of voice, as if with a memorized speech, that he would quickly find someone else. Everything would go swimmingly with him. Of course, they would still be friends, and indeed there were no children to pose any issues.

Max's shining brown eyes searched in vain on the ceiling for something to latch onto. The other customers realized that something untoward had just happened with this couple. It grew very quiet. Eyes stared at him from every table. Max's angular face with the two eyes that were suddenly vibrating wildly on their own impetus looked like a pinball machine with two fugitive balls. He didn't say a word to her, but thought to himself that Cecilia had for years been treating him coldly, like a lady to a greenhorn. She was now already an 'English animal', (*an englishe khaye*, as the Whitechapel Yiddish expression put it), a secretary in the West End, while he had remained at the Yiddish newspaper in Whitechapel, and now even that was gone. Max remembered how his father used to say, with a slight smile, that when troubles come they come like the cars of a railroad train.

The following day, Cecilia took away all her possessions in a moving van. Three husky young men that Cecilia's English lover had hired carried everything away. Max almost never saw her again. She arranged everything with her lawyer and it didn't cost him a cent. The divorce came in the post a few years later.

C.

Max Triebwasser's face grew more and more angular. Deep wrinkles appeared on his cheeks, but his forehead remained smooth, like that of a young man. In his light brown hair, which he had combed back without a part since his Vilna days, white, grey, and silver hairs started to glisten; they created a sort of rainbow effect. He spent his days and nights alone in his flat. He lived decently on the rent money that they paid him for the store below. It was converted into a workers' café at that point. The jolly Italian who ran the café called Max 'Boss'. When he came in, they served him one free cup of coffee after another. He sat in the café for long hours and watched groups of English workingmen eat ham and eggs in the morning and fish and chips in the afternoon, chain smoking cheap, long cigarettes, and making each other break out into wild laughter with their stories of valour and accomplishment at playing tricks on their boss, about sexual exploits, and about bets on horse races. About 5:30 in the evening, they closed the café and Max went upstairs to his apartment.

When it got dark, visions started to torment him. He saw his brother, happy with his stamps and then falling suddenly on the ground like a side of beef in a butcher's shop. He saw his Cecilia undressing and that damned old Englishman starting to wildly kiss her well-formed body. In an attempt to calm down, he would pick up a plate and throw it onto the ground with all his strength. He often recalled how his brother had warned him not to let his wife go to work in the offices in the West End. He grew more and more shabby and let the apartment get more and more messy. The smell of rotten food, a dirty bathroom, and sweaty clothes mixed together in an unrelenting stench.

From time to time, Max would meet his former friends from the newspaper in 'The Cellar,' a large underground coffee-house on Oxford Street next to Selfridge's department store. There they told stories about the good old times when there was constant tumult and rushing around in the editorial offices in the old brick building in Whitechapel.

One after another, his old friends died – they were a lot older than he was. Max began asking the widows and children of his dead friends for manuscripts and books. They promptly gave them to him; that saved them from thinking about whether throwing books out was a sin. It became a ritual among the remaining Yiddish newspapermen in London that after a funeral they started saying "give the books to Triebwasser." Talk among family members of very sick, old Yiddishists came to include the inevitable question of whether the time was coming "to give the books to Triebwasser."

Max took the liberty of building bookcases all around him. The three big rooms in his apartment had high Victorian ceilings. In order to get good carpenters to build in the shelves, he began to dip into the money that his brother had left him. The odour of decay from the books, many of them damp from having been in the cellars or garages of family members before they were donated to Triebwasser, provided a new ingredient for the mustiness.

D.

Max had found an occupation. He made himself the proof-reader of all the books he had in his possession. He perused every word in every book. He began with the last word on the last page, worked backward, and didn't stop till he reached the title page. Wherever he found an error, he circled it with red ink. After that he carefully cut the whole page out of the book with a knife.

He worked in the middle of the night, lying on the floor with the book, fully clothed, by the light of an old electric lamp that was turned on by a button in the middle of the wire. He kept the button near him. Here lay A. N. Stencl's

'Whitechapel, Shtetl of Britain', here I. A. Lisky's 'A Disdained Line of Work' and here was N. M. Seedo's 'Philosophy of Feeling and Thought'. Besides London Yiddish writers, and quite a few volumes of Sholem Aleichem and other Yiddish classics, there were many translations into Yiddish, everything from Henry Thomas Buckle's 'History of Civilization in England' to Rudolph Rocker's 'Pioneers of American Freedom' to D.H. Lawrence's 'Lady Chatterley's Lover'.

He arranged the excised pages in alphabetical order, according to the first letter of the word in which there was a printing error. Where the error was in the very first letter, he rewrote the whole page, with the original inserted according to the erroneous letter and the copy according to the corrected one. If there was more than one error on a page, he rewrote the page again for each error separately. To drive away the nightmares about his brother's death and his wife's betrayal, he began to think he was the proofreader of Yiddish literature, and that the day would come, probably after his death, when the world would recognize him for that.

In the course of working whole days and nights on his floor, he organized a sort of office. On one side were the new books to be proofread, and on the other side were those he had recently finished proofreading. In the front, next to the wire with the lamp-button, lay all the excised pages from the last few days. With time, it became a problem how to maintain in the right order all the excised pages, which cumulatively represented many years' work. At times he considered putting together 'Triebwasser's Lexicon of Errors in Yiddish Literature'. Looking through his back window and seeing a neighbour hanging her laundry on a rope line, he got an idea. He went out and bought rope, clothespins, tacks, and a hammer. He put up ropes in all directions and at various heights. Using the clothespins, he hung packs of excised pages with alphabetical classifications: A1, A2, etc. He began to think that the editor Morris Mayer was sending him compliments from the next world for doing the work so efficiently, and because his industriousness had not gone downhill after Mayer's death or even the demise of the newspaper. Once he dreamed that the Queen of England knighted him for being the best proofreader in Great Britain and the Commonwealth.

E.

'Crazy Max', as they started calling him in Fulham Road, continued his work. New books now came very seldom – his former co-workers and the relevant circles of friends and acquaintances had almost all died.

The neighbourhood began to change. Real estate agents decided jointly that they could make it a wealthy neighbourhood and charge three times as much for a house. They tried to start calling the neighbourhood not Fulham but Chelsea, after the adjacent wealthy neighbourhood. Retirees sold their apartments for a lot of money and bought beautiful houses in the country. Young hot-shots flooded into the area, paying a lot of money to restore the apartments to look as they did when they were built, when Queen Victoria reigned over a considerable portion of God's green earth.

The former residents sold old wooden floorboards and discarded doors, doorknobs, and windows to the young newcomers for a lot of money, and they installed them in place of the newer things that the former residents had installed there. The new phrase for such things was 'architectural antiques'.

Young tenants began coming to the remaining elderly residents and renting rooms from them. These were students, painters, writers, and just plain hippies. The neighbourhood began to seethe with life, with success, and with the youthful drive to remake the world.

Those who rented the café from Max had left. The new residents wouldn't go into the café, with its smell of smoke and fried food. Agents and businessmen began knocking on Max's door. Each one offered him more money than the previous one. Some of them had the money to buy the store below, but that he promptly rejected, because there wasn't enough money in the whole world for him to say an eternal goodbye to the place where his brother had ruled over the stamps and where he had exhaled his last conscious breath. Finally, he rented it out to a young Englishman, an heir who opened a 'wine bar' there to which people came to drink at night, or to generally frolic and look for someone to sleep the night with. Right after he signed the contract, workers began to hammer all day to finish the repairs. The wine-bar opened with a great to-do, and every night it was packed with young men in dungarees and torn California shirts and girls with short dresses and black tights, and sometimes also with hair that was dyed green, red, or purple. Liquor ran like water. They opened the wine bar in the evening, at the time they used to close the old café – it was a gathering place for night-birds.

The boss of the wine-bar felt sorry for the owner, 'Crazy Max', who lived above it. He often invited him to grab a drink of whisky in the evening before the hordes of skirt-chasers started pouring in. Max came in every evening around six and drank down several glasses of whisky all alone at a table, as he used to do with his brother at the same place in the former stamp-shop. When the first troops of skirt-chasers and trouser-chasers showed up, Max promptly fled. Instead of going upstairs again to work on the printing errors, he embarked on long nocturnal walks till three, four, or five in the morning. He walked the streets his lips moving noiselessly. He softly recited from memory errors from long ago and from recently. He created a new daily plan: starting at noon, when he got up, he took down packets of little papers from the strings, and repeated to himself for hours in his room the errors he had found long ago. At about six o'clock, he went downstairs to the wine-bar, and from there he started on his rounds at about seven, seven-thirty, or eight o'clock.

Max Triebwasser walked the streets at night at a slow and steady pace. He walked Fulham Road from its still poverty-stricken beginnings in Parsons Green to its wealthy end in South Kensington. He deviated from his path at every cross-street and walked down that street till he reached one of the parallel avenues, Old Brompton Road or Kings Road, and then turned back to Fulham Road, and he made the same detour at the following cross-street, always returning to the Fulham Road. He fell in love, as it were, with two little streets: Park Walk, with its tall, old apartment-houses, and Seymour Walk, with its wealthy palaces. He stopped for an hour in each of the two little streets, motionless like a standing pear-tree. The whole neighbourhood began to call him 'the night-wanderer'.

F.

During the hour or two in the evening when Max sat in the wine-bar below his apartment, four young journalists who jointly rented a second-floor apartment across the street often came in. They worked in one of the big newspapers in Fleet Street, and like other young 'trendies' they were drawn to the awakening Fulham Road. Just like Max, they came in right after the door was opened, and just like Max, they left when the *bon-vivants* began to come clattering in. Almost every evening, there were only two tables occupied during the early slot when the wait-staff was prepping for the busy night of work ahead. For the first time, Max began to become envious when he watched those four serious young folks, two men and two women. He saw them talking about their work, and even their empty chatter had a certain charm, an importance, a real meaning.

One evening, just one of the quartet came in. He came over to Max and asked whether he could buy him a drink. Max, who always spoke with a loud, clear voice, started to stutter like an infant. After he finished stuttering, he managed to squeeze out a yes, with the gaze of a beggar whom a prince has graciously approached. Max regarded the perfectly tonsured little youth who was wearing a dark green cotton suit with black spots and wore small, round, gold-rimmed glasses.

"You're sure I'm not bothering you?"

"In what way could you be bothering me? I'm sitting here alone, after all. But you always come with three more youngsters."

"Yes – today they all just happen to be busy. We live across the street, directly opposite your flat."

"Really?"

"Yes. Uh, here comes the waiter with your glass of whisky."

"Cheers! To your health! My name is Judd Kingsley. I know that your name is Max Triebwasser. Listen – I hope you will not suspect that we are spying on you, but the window of my flat is precisely opposite the one in your flat, where you work, and I am, how should I put it, intrigued by all the ropes with pieces of paper that are hanging in all directions in your place. Surely you are a researcher and you have found a new way of sorting papers so they will remain in the correct order and at the same time you can see them all and not lock them in a cabinet with drawers. Did I guess right or not?" and he gave Max the smile with which journalists immediately squeeze out whatever information they want from an interviewee.

"No. You didn't guess right. I am a proofreader. What's hanging in my place are pages with errors. I sort the printing errors alphabetically and I know them all almost by heart."

Young Judd Kingsley almost revealed, by a grimace, that he considered the older man plain crazy. But he caught himself in time and began questioning him further in the usual journalistic fashion.

"Are you studying a specific subject?"

"I am a proofreader in all subjects, but only in the Yiddish language. You have heard of Yiddish, yes? Years ago, I worked at the daily Yiddish newspaper in Whitechapel. Did you know that there used to be a daily Yiddish newspaper in London?"

"No. That is indeed interesting. I hope it won't bother you if I write notes in my notebook."

"Write whatever you want. Why should it bother me?"

"The things you are proofreading currently – are they for a printing-house or a university press or privately, for authors?"

"No."

"So, who are they for?"

"For myself."

At this point, the journalist Judd Kingsley couldn't control his eyes, which rolled slightly upward.

"What's bad about proofreading books? One thing I can guarantee you – there are a lot more errors in Yiddish books than in English ones."

"That's really unfortunate. Uh, what will you do with all the errors you find?"

"Nothing. I will die, and the person who inherits my flat will throw them all out."

"Perhaps you can give them all to an institute or a library?"

"What for?"

"So, the errors can be corrected for future readers or new editions."

"What future readers? What new editions?"

"I don't know. After all, I know nothing about that," the journalist stammered.

For a moment, it was quiet. Judd Kingsley gulped down what remained in his cocktail glass and then stuck his pen in his mouth and began thinking about whether he had a human interest article here or not. London had no end of interesting characters one could write a good article about. It occurred to him that perhaps there was indeed something interesting here: perhaps one could interpret this as work toward a philosophical eternity by a person who has lost the community of his language and his work. Max's sharp, penetrating brown eyes seemed to sense what the young man was thinking, and he answered the unspoken question.

"I am not doing my work for anyone – definitely not for the Jews; they don't care about it at all. It's like this: You will agree that a person has to work, yes? Good. How is it my fault that my newspaper closed? How is it my fault that I don't know any other trade? I was the chief proofreader at the 'Jewish Times', which is what our newspaper was called in English. There are no more articles to proofread, so I proofread books. I know every error by heart. It's a shame that you can't read Yiddish – you could test me."

"We'll talk some more tomorrow – I have to go now. Today I am working at the night-desk. May I ask one last question?"

"Why not? Ask whatever you want. I have nothing to hide."

"We see you walking in the street all night, sometimes at interesting, late hours."

"I walk and I repeat the errors to myself. I can't just sit all day in my flat."

"OK – thank you very much. Excuse me, I have one more question."

"Be my guest."

"If we're talking about books, not articles, what are the packets of pages that are hanging in your apartment?"

"They are pages with printing errors that I cut out of the books. I collect only errors. Pages without errors hold no interest for me."

"OK, good-bye, Mr. Triebwasser. It has been a pleasure."

"Go in good health."

Judd Kingsley paid for both of them and left hastily. Max Triebwasser sat all alone at the table and fell into a depression. The young man's questions had made him understand that the activity to which he had devoted his efforts all these years was more than just craziness – it was actually insanity.

G.

That night, Max set out on his usual route. For the first time in many years, he didn't think about printing errors. He was burning with both a drive toward suicide and a desire to kill the journalist and was uncontrollably veering between the two courses of possible action. That night he didn't stroll around like a night-wanderer but like someone in a hurry who was afraid he would be late. This time he didn't move his lips and teeth – they stayed pressed together as if glued. He didn't miss a single street of his walking route, but this night he didn't stop for a while in his two beloved little streets, Park Walk and Seymour Walk – he walked along them just like all the other little streets that meet Fulham Road. For the first time in years, he thought about his hometown, Smargon. From his distant childhood he remembered the guy known as Tsale the Lunatic, who used to walk the roads at night and ultimately threw himself into the machinery of a water-mill. All these thoughts led him to the kind of inconsolable depression that one can't climb out of.

When Max got back to his building, he stood still – he didn't go into his home. He then walked farther for a few minutes till he saw an empty house that was undergoing major repairs. With one great shove, he pushed in the thin boards that were covering the entrance. Inside, a weak lamp was burning. He saw a can of paint. He opened it with a screwdriver that was lying nearby. It was red paint. He took the can and went to the entrance of the house across from his house, and with one energetic lunge he covered the front door with red paint. The street was isolated and nobody noticed. For an instant he felt calmer, but the drive to perform an explosive deed immediately returned. He quickly went up to his flat and took as many books as he could hold in his hands and threw them into the street again and again through the window, till he had cleaned out the front section of one room. It was four o'clock in the morning. Here and there a lamp was turned on in a flat, or a head poked out of a window, but no one called the police. When enough books were lying in the street, Max went outside. He threw one book after another at the window on the second story directly across from his workroom – that had to be the room where Judd Kingsley lived. He didn't hit his target with the first few books, and they fell impotently from the brick wall onto the pavement. Then he did hit another window with one book. The windowpane broke into tiny pieces and a girl screamed and went into another room. Right after that, Max hit Judd Kingsley's room. Together with the sound of breaking glass he heard Kingsley's voice. He fell into a rhythm, and after all the windowpanes were broken (a few pieces of glass hit Max in the face, but that didn't bother him) the books flew in through the nocturnal window openings like self-powered missiles. He didn't care that the residents had all gone out of those rooms – he continued to throw.

Within minutes, the sound of a racing automobile could be heard in the distance, with the hum of an engine and the whistle of a siren. Max was not interested. He was already an expert in how to hit a window. With a piercing screech, the smell of burning rubber, and the rattling of automobile wheels, the police car stopped next to Max. He continued to do his thing. One policeman grabbed him with all his strength in both arms and the other one handcuffed him in the blink of an eye. They stuffed him into the police-wagon and locked the door. It didn't take long for another four or five cars with policemen to arrive. They cleaned up the street, interviewed the four journalists and several dozen other neighbours, and checked out Max's flat, finding thousands of excised pages there, hanging from laundry lines, along with all the books he hadn't managed to throw out the window.

They kept Max in prison till mid-day the next day. The police psychiatrist had a long talk with him in the morning, and then they sent him to the best psychiatric hospital in London, right in Hampstead Heath. There he will live out his life with daily injections of tranquilizers. One sign remains of the night-wanderer: his lips move all night, mutely describing the printing errors of long ago.

Allie and the Wolfman

A.

Jack Wolfman was a skinny little Jew with a bald head and a little beard like Lenin's. His uneven eyebrows and thickish lower lip further accentuated the resemblance. He constantly poked out and drew back his lower lip. That was not one of those involuntary tics – for him it was a sign of status and importance, of dominance over everyone around him.

Every evening, he went to have supper in Carlo's Café in Fulbourne Street in Whitechapel. Though he was not a leftist, he liked it that the café was located exactly opposite the building in which Lenin had planned his revolution during his celebrated visits to England.

His grey suit was frayed. Loose threads hung from the edges of his multicoloured silk tie as if the tie were being unravelled to the raw material – the stuff of cobwebs. Only his white shirt was spotless and freshly pressed. From his walk, it was obvious that this was a man who had been affected by age. He had varicose veins and a truss barely contained his bulging hernia. He didn't believe in doctors and he didn't speak about his illness. When anyone asked him about his health, he answered with one word: "Unremarkable!"

When he was sitting down, Jack Wolfman had the look of a minister or an artist; the 'ability' to appear to be someone who must somehow be world-famous. So that people wouldn't see how he walked, he would be the first to enter the café, in the few minutes when there was practically no one there; the last workers in the district had gone home and the evening customers had not yet arrived. The latter were of two kinds: young medical students and elderly Jews. The medical students, who were completing their studies in the hospital over on the other side of Whitechapel, would take over the much bigger left row of tables in the long narrow coffee-house. The 'Jewish side' was smaller but more charming. The Jewish tables were separated from the large display window in the front, which overlooked the street, by a staircase that went up somewhere. Behind it, next to one of the tables, was a small window through which one could look out at the tracks and trains of the nearby Whitechapel station. The little bench right next to the little window was the 'regular table' of the regular guest Jack Wolfman.

Two large paintings, both of them cheap copies, hung in the café on the wall over the 'Gentile tables', and seemed to smile down at the Jewish corridor. One of them was a painting of a little well amid meadows, with mountains in the distance. The scene was Heaven knows how far from Whitechapel. The second painting was of an exciting show-girl dressed in a leopard-skin coat and nothing else. She showed a deep decollete. On her head she wore a fur hat that hid her eyes. Her most prominently visible feature was her red-painted lips. She too was from far away from Carlo's Café.

The elderly Jews and the young students would converse politely about one topic: where is this Carlo, whose café this is supposed to be? Right after bringing his family over from Italy, he had run away to America with a female medical student. His wife, Marina, had taken a lover that same year, a Jew from Libya, whom she installed as the headwaiter. She had the big sign outside repainted with the name 'Marina's Café'. It didn't help – to this day it is called 'Carlo's Café'. After a few years, when repairs became necessary, she had her former husband's name repainted on the sign – a name is a name and business is business. The Libyan waiter's hair fell out while he was still young. For years he saved money for an operation on the front part of his bald pate. The sewed-in packets of hair, however, didn't take, and he was left with a row of wound-like islands of hair above his forehead. He didn't let anyone pluck them out, hoping that in the end they would blossom into a beautiful head of hair, like that of a young man, as the 'trichologist' who operated on him had promised.

Jack Wolfman, on the other hand, was happy with his bald pate. Not an evening passed in the café that he didn't good-naturedly berate the Libyan about why he kept search-ing for new hair, when a bare head showed masculinity unre-strained by youthful hesitation. Wolfman himself had his pate trimmed every week by an old Whitechapel barber who was an expert on polishing pates so they would shine, no stubble would show, and no unsightly things would develop.

Wherever Jack Wolfman went, he carried two old, brown briefcases. They were stuffed full – it looked as if the locks would burst at any moment. Given his problems with walking, carrying the briefcases added to the unforgettable image of this man struggling heroically on the streets of the East End.

It was a cold day. The big display window of the café was covered with streaks and steam. Jack Wolfman sat down at his regular table near the little window that overlooked the tracks. He rubbed his hands and kept looking down at the two briefcases on the floor, though his feet encircled them under the table in any case.

The Jews who were eating supper in the café, all writers, readers, 'men of culture', or pretenders to one of those titles, thought that Jack Wolfman was just plain crazy. They gave him a name, 'The Wolfman'. To them, that ended it; they didn't call him anything else. He himself happened to like the name very much; to him it was a sign that everyone was afraid of him, as they would be of a wolf. It also distinguished him from the *hoi polloi* in the coffee-house.

Again and again, the Wolfman told them that they had considered him the king of Yiddish poets in prewar Vilna. The critics had crowned him the 'Poet Imperator'. On one literary evening, he recounted, they had almost come to blows over who would introduce him to the audience. Young beauties used to wait for him at the gate of the courtyard on a broad avenue where he lived – it was in fact called *Breyte gas* (Broad Street). They just hoped to say a few words to him and ask him to autograph a book in his style, with a little picture of a wolf that extended from the *'lange-nun*' of Wolfman. They translated his work into Polish, Russian, and

* The final letter of the Yiddish spelling of Wolfman.

German. He recounted that he was the only Yiddish poet in town who could pull proper speaking fees. He said it pained him that none of the other Whitechapel Yiddish literati were from anywhere near Vilna. They were all *Poylishe* or *Galitsyaner*.

The fact that they didn't know his work in the café was, to him, a sign that the people here were doodlers, scribblers, nothings, who even before the war had been far removed from real literature. He never tired of telling how Pilsudski once wanted to make him the Poet Laureate of Poland, but small-minded, jealous Jews sabotaged him with little tricks and denunciations and dropped hints that – secret of secrets! – he secretly sided with the Communists.

In the coffee house, they got used to talking about the Wolfman as if he were a third painting on the wall. They had no patience to listen to his stories again. That too didn't bother him.

Satisfied with himself, he would stare through the little window at the trains, as if he were drawing inspiration for a poem from them. If he joined in the conversation with a word, they would bark at him about why he hadn't ever published a single poem anywhere in London. They said that he carried Shakespeare's sonnets, like underwear, in the briefcases he carried around everywhere.

Nevertheless, everyone in the neighbourhood developed a strong desire to find out what was actually in the briefcases. Wherever he went, he kept them with him. They said in Whitechapel that of course he slept with them in his bed.

B.

That evening, there were fewer people than usual in the café, because of the cold weather. They warmed themselves with cups of cappuccino, around which they wrapped their hands. The Libyan waiter brought in six cups at a time, three in each hand, one on top of another. Nothing ever fell out of his hands. One of the medical students, Alistair McNally – they called him Allie McNally – was sitting alone at a little table. His close friend hadn't shown up that evening. He had long been aware that people hardly said a word to the man who looked like Lenin. He mustered up his courage and invited him to come over to his table, "so he would have more room for his briefcases". Allie came from northern England, a thin fellow of middling height, a longish face, blond hair, and small, round, gold-rimmed eyeglasses. The Wolfman yelled out loudly; *"Ja"*. It seemed that for the first time since Carlo's Café had come to Fulbourne Street, someone had crossed the barrier represented by the aisle between the two rows of tables.

The Wolfman summoned up the strength to take the short walk with big strides. The intestines in his hernia, however, refused to oblige him even in his time of need. In addition, he was encumbered by the two briefcases. Allie saw that the old man wouldn't mind if someone helped him with them.

There was a momentary silence among the Jews. They were resentful that a young man from the student group had invited the Wolfman to his table and not someone else. The

* "Yes" in German.

grimaces on everyone's face showed how they begrudged him that. The naïve young man would believe everything yet. How should he know that the Wolfman was a crazy man who constantly went around with his briefcases and told stories about Emperor Shmemperor, or, as he would put it, Imperator Shmemperator!

Allie McNally ordered some fresh, hot coffee for his new friend, who stretched out a warm hand to him and introduced himself.

"Jack Wolfman. They call me 'the Wolfman'. You can call me just Wolfman, Jack is not an interesting name – fooey! Besides, it should be Jacob. But why talk about it? Just Wolfman!"

The young student was slightly perplexed. "Allie McNally. I have no other names. Allie is short for Alistair."

The Wolfman laid a fatherly hand on Allie's arm and asked him to tell him his life-story 'on one foot'.* The Jew's hand overcame the English medical student's reticence before a stranger. Allie told him his whole story. His parents had died in an automobile accident when he was six years old. A rich branch of the family had adopted him. His stepmother had been unable to bear children. She amused herself by adopting children, six in all, all of them five or six years old. She had no patience for infants. She eventually lost interest in all the children she adopted. He himself had undergone an

* An expression based on a story about the great rabbi Hillel, who was asked by a skeptical non-Jew to explain all of the Jewish religion in the time that he could remain standing on one foot. Hillel's answer was: "Do not do unto others what you would not have them do unto you – all the rest is commentary".

operation for a heart defect in his childhood and was none too healthy. Not long before, he had fallen in love with a nurse, who had recently sent him a letter from Paris telling him that she was going to stay there for a year or two.

"I'm your friend, Allie. Give me that letter and I'll tell you right away whether she has left the door open for a further relationship. The Wolfman knows."

Allie looked around. Seeing that the Jews were again conversing among themselves, he took a folded letter out of the pocket of his corduroy trousers. The Wolfman read it and delivered his expert opinion to his friend, for whom he had already started to feel a kind of paternal friendship, that he, Allie should take a vacation from girls for a while and then fall in love with someone else – with this one it was all over. With a nod of his head, Allie agreed, and then made a face that meant he wanted to change the subject. He gently asked Wolfman how many years he had been in England, in order to get him to tell about his life. In pre-war Vilna, the Wolfman told him, he was a Poet Imperator. His brothers and sisters had been killed. He carried his poems around in his briefcases. He had never married, but when he was young, he had fallen for a different girl every day.

"How else?" he asked his young friend rhetorically. "Would you want to be tasting the same piece of bread every day?"

Everyone had left. The two friends continued to sit at their little table till the coffee-house closed. The elderly Jew and the young Englishman were already 'blood brothers'. Jack Wolfman invited Allie McNally to his flat for a drink.

Allie tried to walk with an old man's gait, so they could

walk at the same pace and the two-generation difference between them would not be visible. Wolfman's apartment was on the other side of Whitechapel, in Fieldgate Street, actually not far from the dormitory in which Allie's room was located. They crossed Whitechapel to Turner Street, a little street that led past the hospital, and then went on to Stepney Way, which in typical London style becomes Fieldgate Street. The walk, which took a long time because of the Wolfman's slow pace, was filled with the timeless, unrushed joy of new friendship.

At the end of the walk, the Wolfman permitted Allie to carry the briefcases up the narrow staircase that led to his apartment on the second storey. The corridors in the building were crumbling and mouldy. Inside the apartment, however, things were clean and carefully arranged, with old-fashioned taste. Pictures of writers and actors were hanging cheek-by-jowl on one wall. On a second wall, there were bookshelves up to the ceiling. On a third wall, there hung rugs like those one finds laid out on the floor. The fourth wall consisted of three large Victorian sash windows, each with twelve windowpanes.

The Wolfman poured two glasses of fine old wine and taught his young friend a Yiddish expression: '*L'chaim*'. Encouraged by the unexpected closeness and by the excellent wine, Allie finally asked his host about poetry. The Poet Imperator grew even more animated. He gave his young friend to understand that a Jew telling a story can't start with himself – he has to start with his grandfather. His

---

* A toast: "To life!"

grandfather, he said, was a rabbi and an author. His father departed from religion and became a teacher in a modern Hebrew school; he also composed Hebrew songs. He, Jacob Wolfman, went over to the folk-language, Yiddish. He even got rich before the war from the fees for his translations. He remained in Vilna till, one day after Hitler's invasion of June 22, 1941, a group of his admirers led him deep into Russia, far beyond where the Nazi armies were expected to get to.

The Wolfman told more and more about his glorious years in Vilna. He constantly refilled the glasses. Finally, there was a long silence. The pause, however, was by no means awkward. The atmosphere was like that between friends. The quiet moments were filled with the joy of sitting near one another. In the peaceful-idyllic fog from the fine old wine, Allie kept thinking about what had become of Jack Wolfman. In Whitechapel, you didn't find successful men around every corner. The Wolfman realized what his young friend was thinking. He began to make excuses for things: Hitler had wiped out everything, killed everyone; those who by chance survived were not the same as they had been; it wasn't appropriate for a serious poet like himself to publish his poems in their little magazines, where any scribbler becomes a 'writer' just because he wants to; if something should happen to him, they would translate his poems into English then, and the whole world would resound with the works of Jack Wolfman; there was nothing to be gained by rushing such things, and the true writer doesn't care whether his fame is posthumous.

After that the Poet Imperator sat with his young friend every night on the 'medical side' of Carlo's Café. He didn't miss looking out the window at the trains. The Wolfman waited for Allie next to the hospital so the two of them could go to the coffee-house. He no longer minded that everyone could see how hard it was for him to walk, and in any case, his health improved: his veins bothered him less and the hernia permitted itself, more submissively, to be stuffed into the truss. He practically stopped greeting the Jews in the café altogether. They watched with envy the way Jack Wolfman and Allie McNally talked with one another. Some started to think that maybe the briefcases really were filled with great poetry. Or maybe something really valuable. For others, it was important that the charlatan's veils should be removed from his friend's eyes. A rotund Jew who always wore a brown hat with a visor even sought out Allie at the hospital one morning. He told him that in every city where European Jews are to be found, there is one nut who says that he was the king of the poets back in the old country. When a similarly monikered Yiddish 'Poet Imperator', also a nut job with two suitcases that almost became part of the guy's anatomy, passed away in New York years ago, they found just two off-colour lines in his suitcase, translated into English: "I never had a lay in a Chevrolet, but in a Ford—O Lord!" Maybe this one in Whitechapel would turn out to have the same two lines locked up in one of his briefcases.

C.

Weeks passed. The extreme cold finally yielded to the change of seasons. Whenever Allie had a free day, the Wolfman took him several stations by the underground to the Wonder-Park on the Victoria Embankment. The previous century,

Queen Victoria had taken a good bit of land near the Thames to give as a present to her faithful people.

At the beginning of the summer, Jack Wolfman asked a favour of Allie. He was going to go for two weeks to Brighton, by the sea, and he wanted to entrust Allie with the briefcases containing his life's work. As the train was about to depart, they shook hands through the window. On the platform the conductor blew his whistle and the train began to move. While the train was still moving slowly, Allie ran along the platform waving fondly with both hands, as if to the father he never had.

Allie missed his friend, the old Jew who looked like Lenin and who was once a famous poet. He no longer went to the café in the evenings. Without his friend – he called him just 'Wolfman' with his northern England accent – there was no reason to go.

The night before the Wolfman was to return from Brighton, Allie McNally breathed easier. The briefcases were lying closed in the wardrobe. The loneliness had turned into hopeful expectation. The next day his friend was coming back. They would continue to eat supper in the café in Fulbourne Street, and afterwards head out for a drink in Fieldgate Street, from the inexhaustible bottles of fine old wine, and then he would go home to his student residence hall to sleep the night and get ready for the next day's studies.

D.

About ten o'clock at night, someone began banging on the door of Allie's little room. He grew very frightened. He felt a sharp pain in the left side of his chest, the kind of pain he used to have as a child before they had operated on him. His body was soaked with sweat. He sat on the edge of his bed and couldn't get up. He couldn't utter a single word. He sat there, mute and silent, hoping that the persons banging on the door would eventually go away. From outside, someone suddenly gave the door a kick with all his strength. The lock immediately broke and the door flew inward to the wall.

The first one to come in was Adrian Renton, the leader of a group of pranksters among the medical students. He was a broad-shouldered, strong fellow with blond hair and a face full of pimples. He exuded the nauseating odour of cheap beer spills accumulated over weeks on his clothing. Behind him stood another four boys. Three were students from Adrian's crowd, and the fourth was just a knife-wielding street-thug who had been bribed with a few glasses of beer to come along in case they needed an outsider for 'dirty work'.

Allie remained seated, mute and bewildered, on the edge of his bed. He was in the state of shock that one goes into during a tragedy, when every second engraves itself in one's memory with horrible clarity. He suddenly thought about Adrian's pranks during the preceding months: he had arranged for a medical cadaver to be removed from the laboratory in the middle of the night and placed next to the door of a timid nurse; the next morning, she had started screaming frightfully; the police were called and they made a terrible fuss, but they were unable to catch Adrian and his group in the act. Every night, Adrian would regale his gang in the pub with stories from the hospital: they had performed a prostatectomy on someone, and by mistake they had cut out a few other organs at the same time; another person had received too much ether and had died; then there was the chap who had the wrong testicle amputated. When the pub closed, Adrian and his gang would go to his room to continue their carousing. First, they would all go and change their clothes. They would put away their ordinary clothes – to go to Adrian's to drink, you had to be wearing a Roman toga. When all of them were dead-drunk, the girls as well as the boys, they would begin an orgy of sorts. But in the morning, they would all return to their posts sober and awake. They knew just how to do that – they ingested potent pills that were strictly forbidden to the public. It occurred to Allie that Adrian and his gang had waited till the last night before 'that old Polish Jew' was supposed to come back from Brighton.

Adrian was the spokesman. He launched into his words with no introduction.

"OK, McNally! Don't play with us! Give me the brief-cases. If not, we'll fix you and we'll throw the briefcases into the river. Don't you know that the Thames is right nearby? Give them to me! Well?"

"What do you need the briefcases for? They're locked. The man's writings are not even in English."

"Shut up and give them to me, McNally!"

"I'll give you money so you can go have fun somewhere else. Here – take it! Leave the man's briefcases alone! What has he ever done to you? What?"

"If we want your money, we'll take it! Who needs your money? Are we gangsters? Listen to him – money!"

"Joe!" he yelled to the street-thug. "Get to work! You can throw his underpants on the floor. A fine doctor he'll be, that one. One drop of blood and he'll faint. I always knew he was only half a man! You won't find any condoms on him – his girlfriend has run away from this hero. She's gone all the way to Paris; Manchester wasn't far enough away for her!"

Allie cringed like a little boy. He sat helplessly on the edge of the bed. His thoughts turned spontaneously to his few recollections of his own parents, to the automobile accident. Everything that was passing before his eyes was worse than death – to him, death was not such fearsome thing, for at the age of six, he had seen his parents lying dead, and now not a day passed when he didn't see death 'from both sides of the fence': the dying patients in the hospital and the bodies that lay downstairs on autopsy tables, sometimes to be sawed apart with an autopsy saw. To live till tomorrow and then go and tell the Wolfman that he had allowed a gang of drunken ruffians to open his briefcases was something he couldn't conceive. For a moment, a ray of hope crossed his mind that Wolfman would not have to find out what had happened. But it disappeared immediately when he heard someone cutting the leather with a knife. It seemed that for Joe, the street-thug, that was much more macho than tearing out the leather tongue and the little lock.

After the first few cuts, Joe ripped open the briefcase with his powerful hands, with the triumphant air of a Cossack cutting open the belly of a pregnant woman during the massacres of 1648. He turned the briefcase upside down. Dozens of notebooks, large and small, fell out onto the floor. The notebooks were old and yellowed. An odour of mould and dust permeated the room.

Meanwhile, the briefcase-cutter was holding the blade in his mouth. Once he had 'finished' the briefcase and had thus triumphed over the 'enemy', he took the blade out of his mouth and made the first cut into the other leather briefcase, this time quietly and leisurely in order to draw out the pain for Alistair McNally, who sat motionless, sobbing with shame over his powerlessness. Even the ripping of the briefcase with his hands was now going slowly for Joe. Here he was moving his hands as if to rip it, and he hadn't ripped it. He gave an angry slash with his knife and made only a pitiful scratch on its surface. He carved his initials and his girlfriend's initials into the leather, and around them he drew a heart pieced by an arrow. He drooled over every cut as if it were pure gold. He hadn't had so much pleasure from a 'job' in a long time. Adrian and the other three students banged their fists on the wall with uproarious laughter.

Suddenly, Joe was tired of the whole business. All the notebooks from both briefcases were now lying on the floor. Just to stand there in a narrow little room and tear leather all night was not his thing. He looked at his watch and told Adrian that he had to be somewhere else. Nevertheless, he wanted his knife-work to end honourably and in a classy style. He gave one last mighty tear and let out a wild cry. He threw the ripped-up briefcase into Adrian's hands and walked out. Adrian was happy that the job of turning the valise upside down so everything would fall out onto the pile that was already lying there remained for him.

"Yahoo!" he cried, as he poured the notebooks onto the floor.

Adrian bent over and leafed through this notebook and that. He began laughing wildly.

"Wow! Empty pages! Not a single word! Your Polack Jew-boy is *some* writer. The Shakespeare of the empty pages! Maybe one needs Jewish glasses to see what he has scribbled there! A charlatan! Tomorrow, I'm taking it all to the café – let the world know what a liar he is!"

Adrian methodically leafed through each notebook and confirmed that there wasn't a sign of ink anywhere. He threw the investigated notebooks, one by one, onto a new pile in the farthest corner of the room, next to the open window. Now and then a notebook flew out into the night time street.

The whole while, Allie sat motionless on the edge of the bed.

The spectacle became tiresome to the three students that Adrian had brought along. Noting that he was losing the interest of his audience, Adrian looked at his watch and told them he had to leave. He went over to the sobbing Allie and gave him a good-natured pat on the cheek as if he wanted to encourage him, make a man of him.

"Allie, why are you sad? No one has died. We've unmasked that disgusting Jew for you. Clean up your room, it's cluttered up with empty notebooks. What a mouldy smell! Ugh!"

Then the four of them quickly left.

Through the open door, Allie saw other students, boys and girls, standing in the corridor. They had watched the whole scene play out. One of the female students took pity on Allie and brought him a cup of hot tea and told him that the whole thing amounted to nothing – it was all part of a student's life. Adrian hadn't meant any harm; he was just a little tipsy. She went down into the street and immediately found the few notebooks that Adrian had thrown out of the window. She dutifully brought them up to Allie and said good-night.

E.

All night the Christian student grieved over the ruptured bodies of the leather briefcases that had contained the notebooks with the unwritten poems of his dearest friend, the Yiddish poet Jack Wolfman. He, an old man who could hardly walk, had been guarding the briefcases all his life, and he, a young student, couldn't protect them from evil for even two weeks. The next day at twenty minutes past four, the train from Brighton would arrive at Victoria Station. What was he going to say to the Wolfman? What kind of friend is it that lets hooligans cut up his property? More than anything else, it pierced Allie to the heart that his friend would know that he, Allie, now knew that there wasn't a single poem in the two briefcases.

Allie thought of some possible solutions. Perhaps he could get rid of the cut-up briefcases with the empty notebooks and say they had robbed him of everything; that way he could at least salvage the other man's pride. But he immediately realized that it wouldn't work; Adrian and his gang would spread the whole story and the café would ring with it for a long time to come.

Allie lay on his bed till the following day, in a sort of haze of despair, regret, and self-hatred about how he had betrayed the Wolfman though his own foolishness and weakness. The lock on his door was broken, but no one came in. He never closed his eyes, but he wasn't tired.

In the afternoon, he went out without changing his clothes and took the tube to Victoria Station to wait for Wolfman.

The train arrived on the minute. In the crowd of people who got out onto the platform, he didn't catch a glimpse of his friend until the Wolfman called out from afar: "Allie, Allie."

He came running up to Allie. With his young English friend, the Wolfman had always conducted himself in a British manner: just a handshake and that's all. After not having seen Allie for two weeks, however, he kissed him and hugged him. He looked at Allie's face and saw that something was not right – his eyes were burning and reddened from lack of sleep and, in addition, he was crying.

Allie took the Wolfman's satchel, and right there on the platform, which quickly emptied out, he told him everything that had happened. Only one thing he failed to mention – that he knew the notebooks were empty. Allie expected his friend to start screaming angrily and hysterically or to break down in tears. Allie repeatedly told him that he had the notebooks in his room, so no great damage had occurred, thank God. He told him that he would get him new briefcases.

The Wolfman laid a hand on Allie's shoulder and said to him that the railroad station was no place to talk. It would be better to discuss the matter over a cup of coffee. They went out into the street to look for a coffee-house. The Wolfman explained that a coffee-house would probably be crowded and full of happiness. Finally, he liked the look of a little restaurant not far from the station and they went in.

Minutes passed with not a word being said. Allie's eyes gradually cleared. From the increasingly quiet movements of his not too healthy chest, it was obvious that he was breathing more easily. A waitress came over. They ordered two cups of coffee. It was cold tourist coffee, not the delicious cappuccino of Carlo's Café.

Suddenly, the aged Wolfman broke out into a cascade of laughter. He began banging his fist on the table and involuntarily spat out some coffee on the table. His head was drawn backward. The whole coffee-house looked over at them to see what was going on. He gradually came to himself and spoke calmly and slowly with the same serenity as at their night-time drinks in Fieldgate Street.

"Listen to me, my friend! You know what? It's unbelievable! For all the years since I came to London, I've had the feeling that they wouldn't be able to wait till after my death, that they would somehow steal or forcibly open my briefcases. I myself had thrown away the keys long ago, so they'd have to tear them open anyhow to see what was going on inside. You probably noticed that your friend the hooligan found that all the notebooks in both briefcases were empty! There's not a single word there! My real poems are in the bank! What else – an old Jew with crippled feet should go around with all of his poems? What am I, crazy? My dear young friend, listen to me carefully. I want to talk to our Adrian Renton. The Poet Imperator is not afraid of young hooligan medical students in London. Let's go!"

They got up and went down into the underground. Allie, having calmed down, felt his face tightening and his eyes starting to burn again. He tried to keep the Wolfman from picking a quarrel with Adrian Renton. He was struck by the fear that what he had just lived through would be child's play compared with what might happen. Adrian Renton was an evil ruffian and this old, sick Jew wanted to start up with him!

It had never been hard for the Wolfman to guess what was on his young friend's mind. He felt that the best gift he could leave for Allie after his death was a certain boldness, confidence in himself, and an iron will to go on under any circumstances. He wanted to eradicate Allie's fearful submissiveness towards the thugs and gangsters who ran the world. Meanwhile, it was important to him to show off to his young friend that he was not just a Poet Imperator but a heroic Poet Imperator.

When they arrived in Whitechapel, they went to stow the satchel from Brighton in the Wolfman's flat. He took out a new bottle of fine old wine, and instead of opening it with a corkscrew, he showed Allie a trick. With his palm, and a knowledge of physics, he skilfully banged the bottle two or three times on the bottom and the cork shot into the air like a shooting star. Allie drew hope from that, like a little boy who had been convinced that his father really was a magician. The Wolfman's talents seemed to Allie like the inexhaustible bottles of wine.

They sat for hours. The Wolfman kept telling Allie new stories about the distant past. When the grey Whitechapel sunset darkened the view outside through the three large windows with their dozens of windowpanes, the Wolfman realized that Adrian and his gang were already in the pub where they drank the night away – the Red Lion on the other side of Whitechapel. He gave Allie a fatherly clap on the knee and said to him with the strength of a Geronimo: "Adrian Renton!"

As they were walking, the fainthearted Allie continued to be afraid. It was insane to pick a quarrel with a ruffian! When they had crossed Whitechapel, the Wolfman started to walk faster and more vigorously than usual. This time his veins and his hernia obliged him.

In the pub, the air was stifling and permeated with cigarette smoke and the odour of stale beer. This pub, too, was divided in half, but here no Jews entered. The larger part was occupied by Whitechapel bums and poor people, who all spoke Cockney. In one corner were the medical students, not the refined type from Carlo's Café but Adrian Renton and his gang. Allie gently jabbed the Wolfman in the ribs with his elbow and indicated, with his eyes, which fellow was Adrian. Meanwhile, Adrian was busy retelling, for the umpteenth time, his adventures of the previous night.

"A crazy old Jew, a sick man who can hardly walk, has been carrying around two heavy briefcases all his life, says that he is a great poet and that they contain his poems, and what is really in the briefcases? Empty notebooks! And who is his great admirer? Our half-baked twit, Alistair McNally!

He wastes his evening time with that Jew instead of going out with girls. Yahoo!"

While he was speaking, Adrian saw through the curls of smoke that the old Jew and the young student were being conjured by some magician in the pub's haze. The Wolfman was walking in front and Allie was hiding behind him. The Wolfman's hypnotically concentrated eyes drilled through Adrian's bravado in the blink of an eye. He sat there mute. Shame was visible on his face.

The bald little Jew stood motionless in front of the seated, broad-shouldered, blond-haired, strong man with the pimpled face. The more the Wolfman stared at him the more the young hero stared into his glass of beer. The tension was broken when the Wolfman suddenly stuck out his hand to the man who had ripped open his briefcases. His arm stretched out limply. Adrian grabbed the hand like a man drowning in the ocean. His own arm, which had been folded next to his body, seemed to cry out with a newborn submissiveness.

"Dr. Adrian!" the Wolfman was the first to speak, knowing full well that the young ruffian was still far from being a doctor.

"Not yet, Mister. Mister . . ."

"Wolfman!"

"Mister Wolfman, hear me out! We didn't mean any harm. We'll buy you nicer-looking and more expensive briefcases. All of your notebooks are in Allie's room. We were drunk, and we were all dying to know what was going on in your briefcases. We'll make good for everything!"

"My real poems are in the bank."

"You're a fine one! We make ourselves criminals to look at the poems, and you play us for fools!" Adrian had begun coming to himself with a sarcastic tone, but it was sympathetic sarcasm.

"Your gentleman with the knife, a prince among princes that one is, where is he? Doesn't he want to show his valour at the bank? Won't he now show us his courage by holding up a bank? What do you say: he can cut leather in Allie's room but he's afraid at the bank? That hero? Ugh! Young man, once upon a time there were heroes – now there's nothing to talk about."

The Wolfman bent Adrian's ear in a friendly way for several hours. They drank cheap beer. Allie sat there, silent and happy. He was suffused with the joyful relief that Jews express by saying the blessing for having escaped great danger.

A great commotion was going on among the Jews in Carlo's Café. The first thing they heard about was the violence that had taken place in Allie's dormitory room. They cursed Adrian under their breaths, but at the same time they were quietly happy that the arrogant Wolfman had been finally unmasked as a charlatan. Then the news came that Wolfman hadn't had much to worry about, since the 'real' poems were in the bank somewhere. Then the rumour spread that the Wolfman had gone to seek out Adrian in the Red Lion, to scold him, and that in the end they had made peace. Adrian and his gang had bought the Wolfman two brand new suitcases. It was like something out of the Arabian Nights!

Several days passed. Neither Allie was seen in the hospital, nor the Wolfman seen in the neighbourhood. People said that they had gone somewhere. Almost a week had passed when they showed up in the café. Both the students and the Jews were happy to see them, as if they were heroes returning from having circled the moon. With great fanfare, the Wolfman announced that he no longer trusted any banks – that he was now keeping the real poems in the new briefcases that Adrian had given him.

F.

Many years had passed since all these events took place in Whitechapel. One winter evening, I went to take a look at the old haunts. Carlo's Café was still there. The two cheap pictures were still hanging on the wall. The walls and the little tables were the same, but the little window next to which Jack Wolfman used to sit every night and through which one could look down onto the trains in Whitechapel Station had been plastered over. Its outline was still marked by a recess in the wall, however. Of the Jews who used to come there, not a single one remained. The students were different too.

I asked the waiter, a middle-aged resident of Whitechapel, to call over the boss. He too was a resident of Whitechapel. I told him that I was a former regular, and I asked whether he remembered Allie and the Wolfman, whom everyone had known then. He had never in his life heard of them.

I inquired further about what had happened to Marina. He was astonished that I didn't know. The Libyan Jew had left her without a fare-thee-well and had taken up with a new lover, an Englishwoman who used to come to the café every day. Marina had shot both of them in their private parts so they would be unable to canoodle any more. The newspapers had been full of the story. How was it possible, he asked, that I didn't know?

Marina had been in prison for a few years. Now, he continued, she is living alone in an institution for homeless women in the neighbourhood. He showed me where the institution was located, and I went there to find her. The concierge in the lobby immediately let me go up to her room. I hardly recognized her. She looked old, dishevelled, and shabby – nothing like the elegant one-time mistress of Carlo's Café. She was happy to see me and boasted about her revenge on the Libyan.

"No one shames Marina! When I finished with him, the wounds on his head were the best-looking thing about him!"

Finally, I asked her about Allie and the Wolfman. She answered that there was nothing to tell. The Wolfman had lived to attend Allie's graduation, to which others came with parents. Allie continued to work in the hospital. The Wolfman died in his sleep, at home. In the new briefcases, they found just one comical little poem, and in English at that! For several years, Allie used to come to the café alone every evening, and he made a point of sitting on the 'Jewish side' of the café, next to the little window where the Wolfman once used to sit before he met Allie. She had also heard that he had given up medicine and had left to go work on a newspaper in the north of England, but she wasn't sure.